A HOOD LOVE GAVE ME *Life* 2

A NOVEL BY

NAI

© 2019 Royalty Publishing House

Published by Royalty Publishing House
www.royaltypublishinghouse.com

ALL RIGHTS RESERVED
Any unauthorized reprint or use of the material is prohibited. No part of this book may be reproduced or transmitted in any form or by any means, electronic or mechanical, including photocopying, recording, or by any information storage without express permission by the author or publisher. This is an original work of fiction. Names, characters, places and incidents are either products of the author's imagination or are used fictitiously and any resemblance to actual persons, living or dead, is entirely coincidental.
Contains explicit language & adult themes suitable for ages 16+ only.

Royalty Publishing House is now accepting manuscripts from aspiring or experienced urban romance authors!

WHAT MAY PLACE YOU ABOVE THE REST:

Heroes who are the ultimate book bae: strong-willed, maybe a little rough around the edges but willing to risk it all for the woman he loves.

Heroines who are the ultimate match: the girl next door type, not perfect - has her faults but is still a decent person. One who is willing to risk it all for the man she loves.

The rest is up to you! Just be creative, think out of the box, keep it sexy and intriguing!

If you'd like to join the Royal family, send us the first 15K words (60 pages) of your completed manuscript to submissions@royaltypublishinghouse.com

Synopsis

Finding out that her deceased husband and best friend bore a child has Aaliyah's mind reeling. As if that revelation isn't shocking enough, she also finds out she's being released from prison on a technicality. Welcome home signs on the day of release fill her heart with intense joy, but it's short lived as she's also met with a barrage of bullets.

Elijah King is the product of a loving affair that left both his parents dead, so he's been told. This reality that's been embedded in his head causes him to seek revenge by any means necessary, until a turn of events makes him have to pick sides. Will he choose who he knows or who he now believes?

Pam Black has a hole in heart after her daughter is killed by the very person she considered family. Unable to shake the hatred for Aaliyah that's settled in the depths of her soul, she wants blood, even if that means using someone in the Jones family to get it. An eye for an eye, right?

As these families collide, alliances are formed and innocent lives are caught in the middle. In this finale, everything isn't what meets the eye. Someone has to live and some people have to die.

Previously...

Aaliyah

For the next few days I didn't sleep much in anticipation of sleeping on my sleep number, beauty rest, pillow-top mattress at home. May fifth slowly came around and I was walking out of the facility into my new life. I exited the steel door and took a moment to breathe in the fresh air. Down the ramp I saw my family in front of a Cadillac Escalade with a *you free* sign. Although a happy moment, I felt an eerie feeling come over me. I shook it off once Emi ran up meeting me halfway down the ramp.

My baby girl wasn't a baby anymore. Everyone got their chance to hug and kiss me as we celebrated in front of the jail. As we loaded into the truck, I looked in the direction of the parked car across the street. It stuck out like a sore thumb and I'm sure it wasn't supposed to be parked there. As everyone talked I kept my eyes trained on the car that had now rolled its window down. Just enough to point a gun out without being noticed.

"Gun, get down!" I yelled out before the truck was riddled with bullets.

Elijah

"**F**UCK!!!" I yelled out while banging my hand on the dashboard of the beat-up Honda Will drove. "How you fuck that up man? Damn! We was this close to getting them!" I motioned with my fingers. We had been planning this hit for the past year and the fact that it failed had me fucked up.

"Lil' nigga, chill the fuck out talking to me like you crazy!" he barked, picking up speed on the car. "The car was bullet proof. No way neither one of us could've known that." He was right, but that still didn't make me less tight. I wanted to kill at least one of the people in the truck to avenge my mama and daddy. An eye for an eye.

I took a moment to call my gma and let her know things didn't go as planned. Of course she didn't take the news too well. She had given us specific instructions and although it wasn't our fault we didn't complete the mission, she wasn't gonna see it that way. My gma was a hard ass. She'd been that way since I could remember. My name is Elijah Meek King. I'm fourteen years old, but one would think I was eighteen or nineteen by how tall I was and how I carry myself.

I had been living with my gma ever since I was born. Growing up, she told me about my parents, more so my mother. She told me what she could about my pops. According to her, he didn't want me but had feelings for my moms. It wasn't until my thirteenth birthday that she sat me down and told me about their deaths and who was responsible for it. Shit was fucked up man. How you kill ya husband and ya best friend? This bitch Aaliyah was ruthless.

"Yo, my gma want you to drop me home." Will sucked his teeth and drove in the direction of my house. We had to come up with another plan. There was no way I was letting Aaliyah see another year breathing. Opening the door to the apartment, I walked past my gma in the living room and went straight to my bedroom.

"Boy, bring yo' ass here. Don't walk through my shit and don't speak."

"Gma we spoke when I woke up this morning," I joked, trying to lighten the mood. I knew she was 'bout to get on us about earlier.

"Do it look like I'm in the mood to play?" She stood up and walked over to me.

"No ma'am."

"Okay then, stop fucking playing. Now come sit down and tell me exactly how this shit went down." Will and I did as she asked. He was riding just off the strength of being my mama's ex. I let him have the floor since he was the one doing the shooting.

"Look, everything went as planned. I did what I said I was gonna do. Like he told you over the phone, the truck was bulletproof, end of story." I could tell he was getting tight having to explain himself again. Gma just stared silently. The shit was intimidating as hell, but from what I knew about Will, he didn't scare easy.

She picked up her jack and Coke off the table and sat back on the couch. "So how many shots did you let off?" He looked at me with a look that asked if she was serious. I shrugged my shoulders, knowing it was best not to question her.

"You didn't give me instructions to count Pam," he responded sarcastically.

"I'ma give you another shot at this shit. Right now I'm sure Iman has his people looking into who took shots at them. I need you to go about your regular day to day for the time being. I'll have Eli reach out to you when I'm ready for you to suit up again."

"No disrespect Ms. Pam, but I'm feeling like you tryna lil' boy me. You can't give me another shot at shit. Remember I'm the one who came to you about this whole set up, not the other way around." I scooted over from Will in case gma decided to pull out some shit from the couch and throw it at him. She was famous for catching me off guard with that shit.

"Will, darling, I know you think I'm just a mother trying to avenge her daughter. Unfortunately for you, I'm also the bitch that makes it possible for you to still eat in these streets. I'm Pam motherfucking Black, watch how you address me son." She stood up, smoothing out her silk robe. "Grandson, let Will out for me please." We both watched as she walked away, glass still in hand. I knew he wanted to say more but didn't want his money to dry up so he tucked his tail and I walked him out like instructed.

I knew my gma probably needed a moment to herself so I went to my room. Even though my parents weren't around, I didn't let that hinder me from living my life. I wasn't the kid that was out getting in trouble over dumb shit. Nah, my gma wouldn't allow it. I was a straight A student at Kipp Academy Middle School by day and a student of the hard knocks by night.

She had been grooming me to eventually take the seat next to her in the drug empire that had been rightfully given to her after my grandfather passed away. Most people thought it was Black's right-hand man Cook that was running the show, and my gma liked it that way. She said the less people knew about her the better. To the outside world she was a widow who was left a heavy lump sum of money, but in reality she was the boss.

Throwing on my Beats headphones, I got to finishing up my science project that was due in two days. I couldn't get focused though; my mind kept going to my parents. I always wondered what it would've been like growing up with my mom and dad. From what my gma said, my mom was very much in love with my dad and he cared for her. Even though he was married to his wife. I had gotten to the last part of my project when I thought of an idea that was sure to get the revenge we so desperately wanted.

Snatching my headphones off my head, I went down the hall to her room. Knocking on the door I waited for her to open it. She did and her eyes looked as if she'd been crying. She went through these crying spells often. Little did she know for every tear she dropped somebody had to pay.

"What you need grandson?" She stepped back to let me in.

"So, I have an idea for how we can get at Aaliyah. This time no guns needed; at least not initially." She nodded her head for me to continue. "I was thinking I could get close to her."

"Not an option. What else you got." She shut me down quick. I was gonna do what I wanted in the end. I at least wanted her to hear me out.

"Hear me out. I could get close to Aaliyah and her family; you know, make her think that I forgive her for what happened. You saw how she looked when we went up there to the jail. She was shocked and sad, like she wanted to get to know me." Gma sat at her vanity in deep thought. I knew my idea would work. If I had her blessing I wouldn't have to sneak around.

"Okay. I'm gonna let you do this, but if I feel like you're in too deep I'm pulling yo' ass out," she said with finality. I smiled big knowing I had gotten my way. "Come here boy, witcho charming ass." Meeting her halfway, I leaned in to give her a hug. She squeezed me tight before letting me go.

"I love you gma. I promise I'm not gonna let you down."

"I know baby boy. We doing this for ya mama, she didn't deserve that shit." Seeing her cry only further fueled the fire burning in me.

Pam

The night I was called to the hospital for Erica I thought she was going into labor. Instinctively I thought it was going to be a happy moment. Nobody could've prepared me for the news I received when I arrived. I was told that Erica passed. She had suffered hemorrhaging in the brain after blunt force trauma. Meaning somebody had done their best to bash my baby's head in. Seeing her body in the hospital's morgue, her eyes were swollen shut and bruises covered her beautiful face. My legs threatened to give out beneath me, but I held it together as best I could.

I could've given up right then and there, but I knew that my grandson needed me. He had been a fighter sense birth. Born a month and a half early he had a brief stay in the NICU. Once he put on a good amount of weight he was free to go home with me. Oddly, during the whole ordeal Aaliyah didn't come around not once. I knew all about the break in their friendship and I was also well aware of the affair Erica was partaking in with Eli. I had warned her several times, but I couldn't stop her. About a month after Erica's passing I had found out why both Eli nor Aaliyah had been around.

Aaliyah had killed my daughter and her own husband. I couldn't believe that shit. Will told me she had been picked up and a neighbor of Eli's had placed her at the scene that night. I wanted to ask Aaliyah face to face if this shit was true, but I couldn't go through her, so I went through her dad. That's right, I took my ass right up to Iman's shop. He had his daughter's back of course and didn't admit to anything. I saw right through his ass. Right there the line was drawn in the sand. Had Black been alive he would've shot the whole fucking shop up. I had other plans though.

I raised my grandson with all the love I could give plus more. He was such a good kid, smart as hell. He caught onto everything and you couldn't put nothing pass his lil' ass. I made sure to be at every court date for Aaliyah's trial. I wanted her ass to look me in my face so she could see how she broke me. I knew if she had gotten off with those charges I was liable to shoot the bitch in the head soon as she descended the courtroom steps. Lucky for her, the jury found her guilty and she was able to live a couple more years.

Yea, I got the measly ass check her father sent, but like I told her at the jail that shit didn't make up for my loss. When Will came to me and told me how he had heard she was being released, I immediately went into planning. If I had to bury a daughter so would Iman. I had planned the hit down to the exact time, but like Will mentioned, no one could've predicted that Iman's car would be bulletproof. I knew we would have another chance, so I wasn't gonna be dumb enough to try to hit her again so soon.

Now that I had a moment to sleep on Eli's idea, I felt it made sense. I wasn't trying to send my grandson on a dummy mission, so I planned to give him all the game he needed to make sure he came out on the other side of this alive. With so much of my attention on my revenge, I hadn't been in the hood to check on traps and get with Cook about the business. When Black was killed I didn't expect to be left as the executer of his estate nor heir to his throne. Granted we were still married, but I couldn't have made it any clearer how much I despised his ass. I tolerated him for the most part.

It was a smart decision on his part. I was really the brains behind his operation anyway, well up until I started playing in my nose. Cook was the muscle so it was easy to keep things afloat. I did the thinking and he did the enforcing. Don't get me wrong, I'd pull my nina out if I had to. I had people for that though. Parking in front of the warehouse where we ran the day to day operations, I strutted through the building into Cook's office. My YSL boots made each step I took that much more sexy. Knocking on Cook's door, he didn't answer. Putting my ear to the door I heard moaning.

"This nigga here," I said aloud. I just knew I was going to walk in on him in a compromising position. "Knock, knock." I twisted the knob and the door opened.

The girl he had bent over his desk tried to get up, only for him to push her back down. He looked me right in my eyes as he stroked her.

"I'm not interested. Get this girl outta here so we can talk man." Like the clown he was, he laughed and let her up. I knew I wasn't sitting on any of the furniture he had in this bitch. Holding my Birkin bag in front of me, I looked on while the girl picked her clothes up from the floor and scurried off.

"You just hate calling before you stop by huh," he said while pulling his pants up, remaining shirtless.

"I don't hate it; I just don't see a reason to. Shirt please, and open up the window in this bitch. It smells like catfish and Bath and Body Works." He chuckled before cracking the window and sitting down.

"So to what do I owe the pleasure of this visit?"

"We need to run the numbers. It was either meet up for lunch or pop up here and since yo' ass don't have no sense of time, I came to you." Pulling out my iPad I went to my Microsoft XL app so that we could go over the month's take. I had to be on top of Cook or our whole business would go under. After running through everything, I stood and got ready to make my exit.

"Aye, I heard Aaliyah got out yesterday. How's Eli doing?"

"As good as expected. How'd you know she was home?"

"I know people who know people." I didn't even care to have him elaborate. Grabbing my Apple pencil from my bag, I had him sign his electronic signature on the numbers we crunched and was on my way. I never hung around the warehouse; it wasn't a boss move. I came, made sure shit was moving smoothly and went on about my day. With business out of the way, I went to drive by Erica's old apartment, something I did often whenever she was on my mind.

Even fourteen years later I felt like I'd just lost her yesterday. A parent should never have to bury their child. Feeling myself about to cry I shook it off and drove off. I had no destination in mind but ended up at the cemetery. I needed to let my baby know that her son was doing great and we were going to see to it that Aaliyah paid for what happened to her. I made sure my baby had a nice plot next to her daddy. Her picture was engraved on her head stone for all to see.

"I didn't expect to see you here." I turned around with my hand in my bag, grabbing hold of my gun. Seeing Aaliyah in the flesh decked out in designer shit made my blood boil. My hand started to shake uncontrollably.

"Bitch, you got some nerve coming here."

"Pam, I come in peace." She held her hands up. I'm guessing to show me she didn't have any weapons. I knew better though. Iman Jones wouldn't let his daughter come out unprotected. It didn't matter that she was now a grown ass woman.

"What? You came here to make sure she was dead?"

"I didn't mean for this shit to happen. Do you know how the fuck we got here?"

"Yea, you killed my fucking child!" I yelled, getting closer to her face. She didn't back down. In fact, she moved a step closer to me.

"Your fucking child was sleeping with my husband. And don't give me the look like you didn't know. Am I using that as an excuse for killing her? No. But I didn't mean to kill her." She had the nerve to let a tear fall. "She had a baby by my husband, Pam. She was my sister and she did me dirty."

"Well I guess you got her back for that, didn't you?" Looking her up and down with disgust, I shoulder bumped her and walked out of the cemetery. In my car I sat and watched her stand in front of the headstone with her head down. "Yea, you gonna need all the prayers you can get," I said aloud to myself before starting my engine to pull off.

Back home I went straight to my bedroom for a much-needed shower. That encounter just let me know that I needed to get this plan with Eli moving. Aaliyah didn't care about killing Erica. Her defense was and will always be, she slept with my husband. I wouldn't give a damn if she slept with her damn daddy. I showered and laid down for a much-needed nap.

"Babe, babe." Feeling myself being shaken, I woke up to find my boyfriend Tim standing over me. We had been dating on and off for a couple years and had recently got it right. Well, at least we were working towards it.

"Hey handsome, funny to see you around this time." I reached up so that my lips met his and kissed him.

"Yea, I worked forty-eight hours straight. This is my first off day in the last two weeks." Tim was an ER doctor at New York Presbyterian Hospital. We had met the night that Erica passed. He was the one that saved Eli. That night I gave him the tightest hug for saving my grandson and also thanked him for doing the best he could to save my daughter. After the whole ordeal, he checked in on me when I visited with Eli while he was in the NICU and as time went on our relationship blossomed from there.

"I know, I've been counting down the hours. Let me run you a bath, so you can relax." Climbing out of bed I kissed him once more before stepping out into my bathroom suite to set up the tub. Both of our jobs were so taxing, half the time we barely got to see each other. Between running a drug empire and tryna get payback, I had forgotten the last time we had sex. "Babe, you're all—" I was cut off by the sight of him naked.

My lips formed a sneaky grin as I removed my wet hand from the water. Tim was so damn fine and very fit for his age. He was forty-six and had the body of a thirty-two-year-old. Thanks to clean eating and alkaline water. I wasn't too bad myself. At forty-five I was blessed to still have my modelesque looks. Removing my slip I revealed my shaved pussy.

"I'ma 'bout to fuck you into a coma," he threatened, making my clit jump.

"Oh, promises, promises." Pulling me into him, he kissed me roughly. My nipples hardened at his touch and aggressiveness. I liked that rough shit. Not breaking the kiss, he backed me up against the sink where he picked me up and placed me on the edge. I got excited in anticipation of his dick stroking my moist center. Tim was well endowed and was bound to hit spots that I didn't even know existed. Starting slow, he guided his dick into me. I felt myself being stretched, and what a good stretching it was.

"That's it baby, you got it, take this dick," he coached me, giving me inch by inch until he was able to get all nine inches inside. "Shit, this is the best place on earth." Appreciative of his compliment, I raised my leg and placed it on the sink giving him space to rearrange my insides. Seeing the change in position as a challenge, he drilled my pussy, causing my essence to drip on his pole.

"Arghhh, fuckk, yes, yes," I panted with my mouth wide open at the way he was doing me. "Ohhh fuckk, shit yea." Pulling at his head, I grabbed hold of his lips with one hand and played with my clit with the other. Kissing him roughly, I felt another orgasm rip threw me causing me to bite down on my lip, careful not to break the skin. My body shook as my pussy contracted in a good way. Looking at the mess I made on him, I smiled.

"I'm glad you got yours. It's my turn now." Pulling out, he turned me over and made me touch my toes. Even at my age I was very limber, so the request was nothing for me. Doing as he asked he entered me from the back, hard. I couldn't make out the words I was saying as he fucked me so good I started to drool. WHAP! "Where you going? I need that pussy right here," he demanded, smacking my ass. I complied, allowing him to hold onto my waist and drill me into another orgasm where we came together.

"Shit, I needed that." I stood up to kiss his lips again then his cheek.

"Me too. I'm gonna get a change of clothes. Make the water warm again so you can get in with me." Tim had me singing, *what a man, what a man, what a man, what a mighty good man.* After rewarming the bath I laid in his arms as he told me about his day. I never told him about my work; for all he knew I was retired and had monies that my ex-husband left me. I intended to keep it that way. See, Tim was a square, with a smidgen of hood in him that came out in his conversation only. Other than that, he was as straight as they came.

"Your job is exciting, but sad at the same time. The fate of people's lives are literally in your hands. I don't know how you do it."

"I took an oath as a doctor. I may not save every life, but I vowed that my success stories would be higher than my fatalities." After washing each other from head to toe, we got out and he went to start on dinner just as Eli was walking in. "Wassup smart guy," he greeted Eli. He had been calling him smart guy for years since Eli was a whiz with anything electronic.

"Hey Tim, hey Gma. What y'all in here cooking up?"

"Just a quick chicken salad. I'm too tired to chef it up tonight. You want some?"

"Nah, I ate, thanks though. Gma, can I talk to you for a minute?" He nodded his head toward the back where I followed him as he walked off.

"Everything okay?" I asked with concern-filled eyes. I was Grandma Shark when it came to my grandson, so if he was fucked with I was sure to bite.

He laughed at my facial expression before responding, "I'm good Gma, put the claws back."

"Boy, shut up." I swatted at him. "What you call me in here for?"

"I wanted to know if I could start that mission I was telling you about within the next two weeks. I know you want Aaliyah to get comfortable enough to let her guard down, but we don't want a lot of time to lapse either."

"Look at you, tryna tell me how to move. Well, let me have a seat and you tell me exactly how you want to carry this plan out. A plan that better not include a hair on your head out of place or I'm tearing the whole city up." I took a seat at the desk he had set up in his room which was his mom's old bedroom. Listening with an open mind, I let him give me a play by play of what he wanted to do. By the time he was finished I was smiling. The plan he had, covered each scenario I had of things that could possibly go wrong. He had crossed every T and dotted every I. We were coming for the Jones'.

Aaliyah

Two weeks later

It's been two weeks since my release and although happy to be out, I was still tryna figure out who tried to take me and my family out. I knew I hadn't had any beef with anyone, well at least no one outside of Erica's family. My dad and Chop had their ears to the streets to see if anyone knew anything. I hated that I may have involved my family in my own beef, mainly my daughter. I made sure to check in with her on the daily until she had to tell me she was good and I didn't need to be the helicopter mom.

"Come on Ma, you ready?" Emi asked, standing at my bedroom door in her Fashion Nova romper and lace-up YSL sandals. Today we were having mother and daughter day. That included blowing money at the mall and pampering at the spa.

"Yea babes, I'm ready." I tugged at my Bermuda shorts once more to ensure they were fully over this wagon I was dragging. My commissary stayed stacked so I had put on a few more pounds in the last few years. All in the right places, of course.

"Yesss Ma, you better serve the people bawdy awdy. They gon' learn today what thirty-six and killing it looks like." She did a little two-step making me laugh.

"Thank you love. Mommy need to lose some weight though. This booty is the devil, it's just way too big." I peeked behind me and shook my head. All this ass on my little body was just uncalled for.

"No Ma, you look good. Come on so I can show you off. You want one of the lieus to drive us or you want me to drive?"

"Emi, you know Mommy loves you. I only been out two weeks boo, let me live to see my next birthday. We need to be driven."

"Oh, you got jokes. I can really drive Ma, but it's all good. I didn't feel like driving anyway. Come on big booty Judy." She went to run off before I could hit her. This felt amazing to be able to have these little outings with my babygirl. We were definitely making up for lost time. Outside, Brandon held the door open to a red, 2019 Audi A6.

"It's so good to have you home sis." He held his arm open to hug me. I embraced him and laughed when he mentioned how different I looked. We drove to Saks Fifth Ave and blew a bag on all kinds of shit.

"Okay Brandon, take us to Great Jones Spa. Ma, you're going to love this, I promise." We pulled up in front of the spa and I could just feel my body relax. Inside, I stood back while my sixteen-year-old gave the receptionist our names for our reservation. It took no time for us to be seen. We both had spa massages that almost put my ass right to sleep. I decided on a simple french mani and pedi once I was done with the massage.

"So, how's school Emi? What them grades looking like?" This was a perfect time to poke her brain.

"All A's of course. Pops, Lou and Ms. Emma ain't playing that." I laughed, thinking about how my dad may have been on her the same way he was on me for years about school.

"That's what I'm talking 'bout baby. Smart just like ya mama, and fine like me too, heyyy." We slapped fives in agreeance. Once our mani and pedi's were done, the next stop was dinner. When we got to Ruth's Chris I looked in the front at Brandon and smiled, dancing in my seat like a big kid. In the restaurant we got a seat in the back and ordered our food.

"Ma, can I ask you a question without you getting upset?"

"You can ask me anything Emi. I can't promise my reaction will be what you're looking for, but I can promise I'm going to keep it one hundred."

"I wanna know about my dad." Feeling a tightening in my chest, I took a deep breath. I knew this conversation would come up at some point, I just didn't expect it to be today. It had been the first time in a while that I had thought about Eli. I wasn't going to be selfish and not tell my baby about her dad.

"Your dad was unique baby. He loved you with every fiber of his being. You were his little chunk butt." We both laughed at that. I went on to tell her how we met and had some blissful years together and how she was made out of pure, unfiltered love.

"Do you miss him?"

I had to think before I answered. Did I miss Eli? The man that turned my life upside down in one night. "I miss who he was." She shook her head and took my answer for what it was and didn't pry.

"Anyone special in your life right now?" I asked, now putting her in the hot seat. The waitress returned with our food and she tried to ignore my question by stuffing her face.

"Oh, we playing the quiet game now?" I snickered.

"There's no one special. I talk to this one guy name Dre, but that's about it." She brushed it off. I let her have this one. We'd have more than enough time to talk about these lil' nappy head boys out here.

The next day I decided to stop by the fashion studio for the first time since I'd been home. The Angels had done a great job at holding things down for me since I'd been away. I hadn't seen much of anyone when I first came home so going into the studio today, I had to look my best. Throwing on a pair of ripped up jeans and a Givenchy t-shirt, I grabbed my purse and slipped on some Givenchy heels I had bought at Saks and was out the door.

I wanted to drive myself around today. Opening my garage door, my face lit up at the white Bentley GT with the red bow on it. My dad was still spoiling me even at this age. I had cut a picture of this exact car out of a magazine while I was locked down and sent it to my dad. I let him know that this was the car I wanted to get myself once I was home. Grabbing the new iPhone XS that Lou had got me from my purse, I called him.

"How's my babygirl?" he answered like I was still a teenager.

"I'm good Dad. Even better now that I found this white beauty in my garage. Do you know anything about that?"

"Can't say that I do, but you enjoy. Somebody must really love you to get you such a gift."

I chuckled at him playing clueless. "Yea, uh huh. I hope that person knows just how much I love and appreciate them," I played along.

"I'm sure they do babygirl. Go take it for a spin and then come by later with my grand and have dinner with us." Agreeing to be over later I hung up and got in the car. Starting it up, I pulled out of the garage and was on my way to Harlem. Arriving at the studio I parked across the street to watch the steady traffic in and out. I couldn't help but be proud of the place. I named it *House of Ice*, using my daughter as my muse. Getting out I hit the locks on the doors and sashayed across the street.

"Aaliyah," I heard someone yelling out my name and turned around to see where it was coming from. Seeing it was Shawn, I stopped once I made it onto the sidewalk. I watched as he exited a Range Rover, leaving it right in the middle of the street with a female in it.

"Really Shawn, really?" the female yelled out the open window, but that didn't stop him from embracing me once he got in front of me.

He hugged me tightly making me close my eyes. He smelled amazing; I knew it was Gucci Guilty for men. Although I was basically inhaling his scent, I didn't return the hug. Not that I didn't want to, but because it was kind of awkward. He and I knew that I was responsible for his cousin's death and although this was a welcoming hug, I knew I still had to be cautious. I still hadn't found out who was behind the shooting a couple weeks ago.

"Man, I heard you was home, but I didn't wanna believe it 'til I laid eyes on you." He stood back, admiring what he saw of course. Beeeeppppp! The horn to his car went off making us both turn around to see the girl leaning on the horn along with a line of cars behind it. "Calm y'all ass the fuck down. Y'all see me having a damn conversation with my ex-wife, take y'all ass around." I bust out laughing at his audacity.

"Really Shawn? Ex-wife though? In your dreams. Go move yo' car and get yo' lady friend before she come over here acting like she don't have the good sense God gave her." This man was still a trip.

"Man, I ain't thinking about that broad. I'ma get rid of her real quick, don't move." I looked at him like he was crazy.

"You think I'ma stand out here in this sun and wait for you?"

"You right, damn man you got me nervous man, it seem like forever." Beepppp! The car went off again. This time it was just the girl. The cars behind his smartened up and just went around, but not before giving him the finger. "Here, take my phone. I'ma call you to see where you at. I'll be back in twenty minutes tops. She don't live too far from here." Before I could protest he put the phone in my hand and jogged back to his car. I watched as he drove off like he hadn't just held up traffic. Shaking my head I went into my studio.

"Oh my goddddd, babygirl!" Keisha yelled excitedly once I walked through the door. The customers looked in my direction and I smiled. Keisha ran over to me pulling me in for a hug.

"You so damn ghetto," I teased, hugging her back.

"Bitch please. Why you ain't tell me you was coming home? Ooh, I'ma kick Brandon's ass."

"Kick Brandon's ass?" I looked at her with my brow raised. She shook her head blushing. "Mmhmm, we'll talk later, nasty. Look at this place though. It's beautiful! You held it down for ya girl."

"I know you didn't expect anything less boo. Come on, let me introduce you to the team and we gon' chop it up in your office." I nodded my head and followed her through the studio. It was an open floor plan with a pearl and white color scheme. The floors were marble with a sparkle finish and the walls the same with mirrors throughout the place. She introduced me to three styling consultants she had personally hired based on their experience and their social media pages. Some other shit I had to learn, Instagram and Twitter.

The team consisted of Brielle, Mia, and Tisha. They were all bubbly and knew fashion like the back of their hands. After getting to know everyone I followed Keisha to the back to my office. I didn't know what to expect when I walked in, being that I didn't get a chance to design it. When I walked in I was blown away. The color scheme was white and gold. The white modern office desk had a lacquer finish, with an S-design bookcase, perfect for storage. The white and gold swivel desk chair paired perfectly. Admiring the bookcase, I saw different design books and magazines. There was also a small sectional off to the side where a snack bar and mini fridge sat. They were even able to get a nice-sized bathroom in there.

"You did yo' motherfucking thing Keisha. I can't thank you enough."

"Girl you don't have to thank me. Between the check you gave for me working here in place of you and the money I'm still making with your dad, I'm more than good. Go sit at your throne boo and let's catch up." I did just that placing the phone that Shawn had given me on the desk. I gave her a rundown of the last fourteen years, including brief snapshots of what happened that night that changed my life.

"Damn sis, I always knew there was something about that bitch Erica. I swear it's always the ones closest to you. That's why I don't even let a bitch get too close to my nigga, not even my sisters. Bitches get too familiar and I'm too familiar with guns, so they need not to try me." I chuckled at her serious expression.

"Right, so speaking of yo' nigga. Girl you messing around with Brandon?" I had missed so much.

"More like about to be Mrs. Case." She flashed her engagement rock along with a big smile.

"Oooh bitch, yesssss. And to think his big head was just driving me and Emi around yesterday and ain't mention shit." I was so happy for my girl. "So, I'm making your dress, right?"

"And you know this mannn," she mimicked Chris Tucker, making us both bust out laughing. We caught up for a few more minutes with her showing me the sales on the new Mac computer that was set up for me. In the midst of her giving me a walk-through of the day-to-day operations, the phone that Shawn left me with rang. Answering, his voice came through smooth like butter.

"Where you at love?"

"I'm in my shop, the one we were standing in front of."

"Oh aight, I'm headed in there in a minute." I hung up and looked up to see Keisha staring dead at me.

"What?" I said innocently.

"Ain't no what. Who was that man on the phone?"

"Oh that was Shawn," I replied nonchalantly.

"Erica's cousin Shawn?" I shook my head yes.

"I know what you wanna say without you even saying it. I'm strapped and moving cautious, no worries boo." She nodded her head confirming that was just what she was thinking. Hearing a knock at the door we both turned around. "Come in," I said to the person. It was Tisha.

"Hey, Aaliyah, there's a guy named Shawn asking for you. Should I tell him to come back or you wanna come to the front?"

"Umm, you can have him come back." I looked at Keisha who shrugged her shoulders before walking out as Shawn walked in. He gave her a head nod to say wassup and she did the same. I motioned toward the couch for him to have a seat while I remained seated at my desk.

"This all you?"

"Yep, it's the first time I've been in it since everything was updated."

"Man, this shit nice as hell. I'm proud of you."

"Thanks, I appreciate that. So, wassup Shawn?"

"Why you say it like that?"

"Look, let's cut this whole I'm happy to see you act. You and I both know where I came from and why I was there. So again, wassup?" I needed to bait out the bullshit now.

"Yea, I know why you were there. It's fucked up that my cousin died, but I know for a fact you ain't put her there on purpose. I know for a fact you loved my cousin like she was ya own blood. I also know she was dead ass wrong for how she was moving. That don't change the fact that I still care about you though." He seemed sincere, but I was still on the fence.

"Somebody shot up my dad's truck the day I was released. You know anything about that?"

"Don't insult me Liyah. If I'm shooting anything it's not to miss." I looked in his eyes and knew he was telling the truth. "Enough of this serious shit man. Can a nigga get a hug and a little feel of that booty. That shit sitting back there looking like a meal." I tried to hide my smile but failed. Standing up, I walked from behind the desk and stood in front of him. Standing up, he wrapped his arms around my waist and my arms instinctively went around his neck. "I really missed you Liyah," he whispered in my ear.

Not wanting him to know I felt the same, I stayed quiet and put my face in his neck. The moment felt so right, but I'm sure the people around us would think it was so wrong. I'm sure I'd find out soon enough.

Emery

I was enjoying every bit of having my mother home. She was truly my best friend. The past fourteen years had been a little rocky without her. Don't get me wrong, my life was good and I had no shortage of love. There was just nothing like a mother's love. Once I got of age to understand why she wasn't around, I slowly started to be okay with the fact that she didn't want me visiting her at the jail. I think I was about ten when I asked my pops why she was locked up and he told me. To say that I was shocked was an understatement.

I remembered bits and pieces of moments with my dad when I was little. I remembered my godmother Erica too. Although I think about my dad every now and then, I understood why my mother felt the need to do what she did. All in all, she was home now and that was all that mattered.

"I really can't wait for this class to be over. Like forreal, I'm convinced Mr. Garrett likes to hear himself talk," my friend Porscha complained like she did every day about our biology teacher.

"Girl, we got thirty whole minutes left, P.O.P hold it down," I joked, and she gave me the finger. We listened to Mr. Garrett drag the class out to the bitter end before the bell rang.

"Oh thank God for small favors," Porscha said aloud for everybody to hear, causing the whole class to bust out laughing.

"Watch it Ms. Bailey," Mr. Garrett warned. I walked right in front of her ass and out of his class. She was always getting called out on some shit. She made it out after the crowd of other classmates and we headed to third period. This was the time when we would get caught up with the junior high school kids. I went to a small school that shared a building with a middle school.

"Aye, King. Come here for a second." Hearing my name called by the guidance counselor I went to her at the same time a boy was headed in his direction as well.

"Oh, I was calling Mr. King, sorry about that Emery." Me and the boy looked at each other and we shared an uncanny resemblance.

"No problem Mr. Scott," I said to the guidance counselor before walking back over to Porscha who decided to wait for me. Taking one last look at the boy, I kept it moving.

"Damn, y'all look alike. He was fine too."

"Bitch he in junior high school. Bring yo' ass on P. Kelly." I cracked up at my own joke while pulling at her arm.

For the rest of the day all I could think about was that kid and how he looked like me. It was weird as hell. By the time we got to the end of the day I was ready to get home so I could tell my mom about it. Giving Porscha a hug, I went to walk out of the building when I was stopped by the kid from earlier.

"Emery, right?" he said with a charming smile.

"Yea, who wants to know?" I asked with my hand on my hip.

"I'm Elijah, Elijah King, your brother." I looked him up and down before laughing.

"Boy you ain't no kin of mines. I'm my mama's only child, quit playing." I went to turn around and head out the door before he stopped me in my tracks.

"But not your dad's." Turning on the balls of my feet, I went back to him.

"How you know my dad?"

"I don't. Never got a chance to meet him or my mama. Her name was Erica." Okay now this shit was crazy. At first I thought he was lying but then he mentioned Erica, my mom's ex-best friend being his mom. Taking out my phone, I quickly snapped a picture of him. "What the hell?" he said, throwing his hand up from the flash that I'm sure blinded him.

"I needed to take a picture of you to show my mom and verify your story. Just 'cause we look alike don't mean nothing. You know they say all black people resemble each other. If it's true I'll come find you tomorrow." I walked off before he could say anything else.

Later that night, my mom and I went over to Pops' house to have dinner with the family. When I got home earlier my intentions were to ask my mom about this Eli kid, but she wasn't there when I arrived. If I did have a brother why wouldn't she tell me? Did she not want me to know? Those were the questions that were going through my mind as I sat across from her at the dinner table.

"What's the matter Emi Ice, you don't like the food?" Pops asked.

"Girl I will slap you clear into the middle of next week if you try to play my famous chicken parmesan that I've been sneaking you since you was eight months old," Ms. Emma threatened, telling on herself.

"Oh really?" my mom said, making me chuckle.

"Oh girl please, don't *oh really* me. Find out what's going on with yo' child. She been sitting here with her lip almost touching the table all night." She managed to take the heat off herself.

"What's wrong boo?" my mom asked, concerned.

"Ma, do I have a brother?" She put her head down, but quickly raised it back up.

"Yes, you have a fourteen-year-old brother." The table got quiet, no one looked shocked though.

"Dang, so everybody knew but me? Why nobody told me all these years?"

"Emi, to be honest with you, I just found out myself about two weeks before my release. He came to visit with his grandmother, Erica's mom."

"Oh, well he goes to the middle school inside my school. He stopped me today in the hallway. Can you believe how much we look alike?"

"I can because he looks just like your dad." I nodded my head in agreement. Feeling a little better that she clearly didn't lie to me about it, I went back to eating my food along with everyone else.

"Now Ms. Emma, back to this chicken parmesan you was sneaking my baby at eight months." My mom pointed her fork at Ms. Emma who snickered.

"Stop living in the past girl." That lady was a trip.

At school the next day, I went to find Eli like I said I would. He was surprised when I stood at the door during his gym period. It was my lunch hour so I was good. He had just made a basket when I clapped my hands causing him and the other guys in the gym to look my way. Calling a timeout with his hands, he walked over to me.

"Good shot, brother." I threw the brother part in there to see if he would catch on.

"I see you got the confirmation you needed." Yep, he was smart, we were related.

"I did."

"Cool. So, how do we do this?"

"Do what?"

"You know, get to know each other since we're siblings."

"Oh, I ain't say we was doing all that. I just wanted you to know that you were right. As long as you know I'm out here in the world and vice versa, we should be all good." I wasn't looking for a little brother. I'd been doing just fine as an only child and plus, who would want to get to know their mother's killer's daughter? Even if we were related. That's a hard pass for me.

"So, what happened?" Porscha asked once I made it back to the table in the cafeteria.

"Nothing happened. I told him we were related and kept it pushing."

"Really Emery? You cold blooded."

I gave her a stank look before responding, "How am I cold blooded? I don't know him like that to be kicking it with him."

"You too smart to be so dumb. That's why you need to kick it with him, so you can get to know him. That's yo' brother girl."

"I'm good. We went all these years without knowing each other so continuing shouldn't be a problem. I don't wanna talk about it anymore." She motioned like she was zipping her lips. If I did decide that I wanted to get to know Eli I didn't want it to be forced. It had to be on my own terms. Putting my Maury situation to the back of my mind, I focused on the fact that today was Friday and Porscha and I were going on a double date with Dre and his cousin Marquis.

Dre and I had been talking for the past six months and he was cool, he just did too much sometimes. Porscha knew she was coming as the buffer between us just in case he did something stupid during the date, I could up and leave his ass using her as an excuse. The date worked out in her benefit because she liked Marquis a lot.

"What movie we supposed to go see tonight?"

"*The Intruder*, text Marquis and see if they bought the tickets already."

"Girl, why you can't text Dre and ask him?"

"'Cause you know I need a couple hours before I'm in contact with him. He has a habit of doing something stupid before we do anything."

"You moody as hell."

"Yea, whatever, just text him." She did as I asked and he responded that they had bought the tickets. Knowing that was secure I went through my phone to check and see if my outfit I ordered for tonight had come in the mail. While searching my email a notification came in with the information on the car that had shot at the family the day my mom was released. The email stated that the car was registered to a Mildred Stanton. Passing the information on to Pops via text, I went on about my day.

Later on that night Porscha and I sat at my vanity putting on makeup and listening to music. We were both dressed and making good timing to be at the theatre as soon as the previews started. Being that it was springtime I was able to dress comfortably in a jean short romper with a crop top underneath. Adding a little Trophy Wife Eye Shadow to my eyes and Fenty Gloss from Rihanna's Fenty Beauty collection, I was ready. Sliding my feet into a pair of Dsquared sneakers I was pleased with my look.

"Y'all look cute," my mother peeked in, complimenting us.

"Thank you," we said in unison.

"Brandon is gonna drop y'all off and be back to pick y'all up around midnight, okay?" I nodded my head in understanding and she walked off. Usually I would be annoyed that I couldn't drive my car, but tonight I was fine with riding. Brandon drove us to Ipic Theatre where we met up with the guys.

"Wassup Liyah, you looking good," Dre complimented me while pulling me in for a hug.

"Thanks. Y'all ready to go in?"

"Yea, I got the tickets." We walked in hand in hand, more like he put his hand in mine and I didn't wanna be rude by snatching away. We sat in one row while Marquis and Porscha sat in another. I took the opportunity to order food while the previews played. Throughout the movie I had to keep moving Dre's hand off my damn thigh. By the time he tried it for the last time, I slapped it making him laugh. I didn't find shit funny though.

I was ready to go once the movie ended. I was highly annoyed and the plans to chill after were now an afterthought. I excused myself and dragged Porscha with me to use the bathroom. It was hard pulling her away from Marquis's ass but I did it successfully.

"Girl, I had just made my move, why you acting like that?" she asked once we made it inside the bathroom.

"I needed a break from Dre's touchy-feely ass. I can't even tell you what happened in the movie because I was too busy swatting his hand." My face was turned up and she giggled. "It's not funny heffa." I laughed too because she was so damn goofy.

"Come on, let's go back out there and ditch them, then we can go back to your house." That's why I rocked with my girl P; she was down for me. She could've easily been on some fuck you I'm doing my own thing type of shit. Instead, she was willing to leave with me. As we were leaving out the bathroom we bumped into a lady.

"Oh, sorry about that," I apologized before walking around her.

"It's okay E... I mean, sweetheart." It sounded as if she was about to say my name. I stopped for a second, we locked eyes and she smiled before walking off. That shit was weird as hell. Finally meeting back up with the guys, I let Dre know that I wasn't feeling well so that I could leave early. I made sure to text Brandon who was out front waiting on us. While Marquis was understanding, Dre, on the other hand, was not.

"Forreal man, you been acting funny all night with the kid. Now you sick, come on Emery." I didn't wanna embarrass him in front of his friend so I pulled him to the side.

"Look, I'ma keep it real with you. I like you, but sometimes you come on too strong and it's annoying. Like that touchy-feely shit you pulled back there, that's not what I'm on." I could tell he was offended but kept his cool.

"That's all you had to say ma. You ain't gotta lie. I like you too and if I'm doing something you don't like you gotta speak up so I can check myself. I apologize, real shit." I was taken aback by his response and it made me smile at his sincerity. He pulled me in for a hug and kissed my cheek. "I'ma let you slide with that sick shit 'cause knowing yo' ass, you already called your ride." We both laughed at the accuracy in his statement. Heading back over to Porscha and Marquis, we left and I promised Dre I'd text him once I got home.

"Hey, Emery." I looked to the side of me to see Eli walking up to me with the same woman I bumped into at the bathroom. As he got closer to me, she walked off in another direction as if she was tryna hide that they were together; odd.

"Hey, wassup Eli. What you doing out this late?"

"I'm grown sis." He smirked, giving a charming smile that I'm sure got him out of a lot of trouble. "Let me go, I left someone waiting for me. I just wanted to say wassup." I gave him the 'okay you said what you wanted to say now get on' nod. Catching on, he walked away.

"How old you think he is friend?" Porscha asked biting her lip.

"Trick he's younger than me and plus, that's my little brother." I playfully shoved her and she laughed.

"Hey, we can be sisters." This girl was crazy.

For the past few days Eli had been popping up everywhere I happened to be at school. It wasn't creepy, but I was a little put off by it. I mean, was he too young to have a motive? I mean, my mom did kill his mom, so why wouldn't he? Today I was feeling nice and decided to find him before he found me. Again, on my free period, I found him in the gym.

"Aye, lil' bro," I called out to him as I walked in and took a seat on the bleachers. I laughed at his facial expression that showed he was shocked. Jogging over to me, he sat a step down.

"What you doing here?"

"Oh, I can't pop up on you like you do me?"

"Nah, I ain't saying that. It's just that whenever I do see you and try to speak you brush me off like I got the bird flu or some shit." He was right and I wasn't doing it to be mean, just 'cause.

"I mean, you did kinda come outta nowhere like, 'hey, I'm your brother.'" That made him snicker.

"Okay, I see ya point. I apologize if I came on too strong."

"It's cool. Tell me about yourself. I've been an only child for so long." I had about thirty minutes to spare so we shared stories about our childhood. Thankfully, neither one of us brought up our parents. That saved a whole awkward moment, thank God. "Well this was a good get to know you moment. What's your number? I'm gonna save it and text you so you can have mine." He agreed and gave me his number. The bell had rung indicating it was time for my fifth period class. Standing up to leave, I gave him a pound and went on my way. Maybe I could get used to the idea of having a little brother after all.

Elijah

I had officially started phase one of operation get back at the Joneses. I had somewhat broken through a wall that Emery had put up. The guidance counselor calling out our names in the hallway a couple days back was a blessing in disguise. Seeing Emery in person, she kinda looked like the female version of me. At that point it clicked that she was Aaliyah's daughter. When I stopped her that day I knew she would be skeptical, that's why I didn't press the issue too much. She confirmed what I already knew the next day.

Today we actually got to talk. She told me about herself, hobbies, and shit like that. Now that she was opening up, it was only a matter of time before I'd be able to get close to the family. Leaving school I hopped in my cousin Shawn's Range Rover. He was my mother's first cousin and would pick me up often and hang with me whenever Gma permitted it.

"Waddup boy? Get yo' lanky ass in here." He was always cracking on my height.

"Man shut up. Waddup, where you taking me?" I asked while dapping him up.

"I wanted to drive around for a little bit. You know, politic witchu for a few lil' nigga. I'll get you something to eat and make sure you get back to ya grams at a decent hour. That cool witchu?" I shook my head yes and he sped off once I closed the passenger side door. Shawn was cool as hell. He worked with my gma's organization too, but unlike Will he was higher up on the ladder. He made his own plays without anyone's insight.

We drove out to City Island to eat at the Crab Shanty. Ordering our food, Shawn ordered himself a drink and we sat outside. He didn't talk immediately just sipped his drink, and I had my face in my phone checking my social media pages.

"I brought you out here 'cause I wanted to pick ya brain about something." I put my phone down to give him my undivided attention. "How you feeling about Aaliyah being home?" Now that took me for a loop. I wasn't aware that he knew that I knew about Aaliyah.

"What you mean how I feel?"

"I mean, how do you feel about the woman responsible for the death of your parents being out?" I didn't know how much he knew about the plan between myself, Gma, and Will, or if he knew anything for that matter. I kept my tone even so as not to evoke any ill feelings.

Shrugging my shoulders I answered, "I don't feel no way. I mean, at some point I'd like to pick her brain about what happened."

"How you think your grams gon' feel about that?"

"She should be cool. I've already been in contact with my sister since our schools are in the same building. That's the only ties I have to my dad you know."

"I feel you. I may be able to help you set that up." I looked at him with a raised brow. What kinda ties did he have with the Jones family? "Liyah and I have always been close. Of course after everything happened with ya moms and pops things changed and we fell off. I had a chance to see her since she's been released though." Ahh man, this nigga was an opp. Here I was, trying to get close to Aaliyah to get revenge on my mother's, his cousin, death and he just wanted to be close to the bitch.

I had lost my appetite at that moment and asked if I could get my food to go. He grew up with my mom and this was a big fuck you to her and me. It was cool though, he was gonna be my other way in. I would use him and Emery as my buffers to get Aaliyah right where I wanted her. After all, who would see a fourteen-year-old as a threat?

I got closer to Emery over the next few months and I had to admit, my sister was dope. We still hadn't hung outside of school much, but I wasn't pushing it. I knew it was best to play it cool and she'd eventually open up, giving me access to the family.

"Hey, what you doing tomorrow after school?" she asked me while we were in the middle of changing classes.

"Nothing, why wassup?"

"You think ya grandmother would be cool witchu coming by my house for dinner tomorrow night? She could come too if she wanted." I looked at her like she was crazy. The last thing she wanted me to do was invite Gma.

"Umm, I don't know about inviting my grandmother sis. She isn't your mother's biggest fan; for obvious reasons of course." I wanted to see her reaction. When she gave none I just agreed to asking Gma to see how she felt about it. Later that night I went to tell Gma about the invitation to Aaliyah's house. Surprising me, she offered to drop me off. She was a little too eager if you asked me.

Friday night came around pretty fast. I dressed casually in a Gucci t-shirt, cargo pants and a pair of Gucci monogrammed sneakers. I sat with Gma for all of thirty minutes while she grilled me to make sure I was quick on my feet with answers to any questions I may have been asked.

"Aight, I think I'm good." I went to stand up only for her to pull me back down. Now she was dragging it.

"Boy, listen to me and listen to me good. This shit ain't no fucking joke. You make one wrong move and end up on a newspaper clipping. Keep yo' eyes open at all times. Remember they're not gonna be expecting a fourteen-year-old to be plotting against them. I need you to tone that confidence down and act like a goddamn child for once." She pointed her finger in my face for me to understand the severity of the situation.

"I got you Gma." She kissed my forehead and we hopped in her car and got ready to make the drive to Emi's house. When we pulled up in front of the address Emi gave me I was surprised to see it was a condo and not a house.

"Ahh, that bitch think she slick," Gma pointed out. "She know damn well she don't live here. She didn't want us to know where she laid her head. Smart move Aaliyah, smart move." I texted Emi letting her know I was out front. She texted me back telling me to come in and take the elevator up to the penthouse level. I showed Gma the text and she shook her head. "Go on in and keep ya phone on you at all times. I'ma find a restaurant close by that I can sit in until you're done."

Giving her a quick hug, I got out and made my way into the building. Giving the doorman my name, he escorted me into the elevator and pressed the penthouse floor for me. The elevator doors opened to a big ass room, where Emi and her mom stood looking out of the floor-to-ceiling window.

"Hey Eli, glad you could make it," Emi greeted me with a smile and light hug.

"Nice to see you again Elijah," Aaliyah spoke in an even tone. "Will your grandmother be joining us tonight?"

"Nah, she had other business to tend to."

"Oh, well come to the kitchen. I had the chef hook us up some stuff. Do you like seafood?" I shook my head yes. "Your mom loved seafood." The mention of my mother made my jaw flex, but I held my composure. Throughout dinner, Emi and I talked while Aaliyah looked on.

"Can I ask you a question?" I decided to pick Aaliyah's brain about my mom to see how she really felt about her. She took a sip of her wine and nodded for me to talk. "What was my mom like?" From the corner of my eye I saw Emi shift in her seat while Aaliyah straightened her posture moving closer to the table.

"Your mother.. your mother was fun and loving. We were friends since kids, so close that I considered her family. In fact, she was Emi's godmother and boy did she love her some Emi." She smiled when she spoke about her and it fucked me up.

"So why did you kill her?" For the first time since I'd been there she showed some emotion. Her eyes got misty and Emi grabbed her hand.

"Your mother was a sneaky, snake ass bitch, that's why she died. Now you can go and tell her family that since they're tryna use you as a decoy to get close to us," Emi blurted out.

"Emery!" Aaliyah yelled in an attempt to shush her. I was stuck and didn't know how to respond.

"Yea, I peeped yo' shit from a mile away. Who in their right mind would be trying to get to know anyone associated with the person who caused them that type of pain?"

"Man, fuck y'all." I couldn't hold back my anger. She didn't know shit about my mom to be talking about her like that. Sliding back from the table I stood to leave. "You killed my parents and said fuck me in the process. You weren't my mama's real friend. You was jealous that your husband fell for her and they made me." I hit my chest with my fist as tears fell from my eyes.

"Fuck this," Emi said before walking out, leaving me and Aaliyah in the kitchen.

"Eli, have a seat. I wanna tell you this and then you can leave if you still want to," Aaliyah spoke in a soft voice. I chose to stand. "Look, I'm not sure what your grandmother may have or have not told you, but this is the real. Your mother and father, my husband, started sleeping together behind my back and it went on for a while. When everything went down that night I had no idea that she was pregnant with you. I didn't find out until the day I was arrested. I'm sorry for what happened with your mom. I promise you it wasn't my intent to kill her. Did I want her to feel pain for ruining my marriage? Yes, but I swear I didn't wanna kill my friend. Now your father took an oath and let's just say, death had to do us part." She stood up and leaned over the table towards me. "Although there's nothing I can do to make up for the loss and you having to go through life without your parents, I wanna make it better now."

I looked at the hand she held out for me to shake and grabbed hold of it. Fresh tears fell from her eyes making my once dry face wet again. I let her hug me as I wept for what seemed like forever but had only been a few minutes. Moving from her embrace, I let her know I had to go. Texting Gma, I let her know that I was ready. Once I made it outside she was out front. Getting in the passenger side, my once tear-filled face formed a smile.

"Checkmate."

"On to the next phase." I now had Aaliyah right where I wanted her. The goal was for her to feel sorry for me and I believe I accomplished that tonight.

Aaliyah

"I don't trust him Ma, I'm telling you," Emi mentioned while helping me and Lou tidy up the shop after a long day.

"What is it that you don't trust about him Emi Ice?" Lou asked as she dressed one of the mannequins in the window.

"Just the way he popped up. You can tell he has an ulterior motive. I mean, it's no way Erica's mother is not planning something now that you're out ma. I'm just saying." I had been thinking the same thing but hadn't expressed my thoughts to anyone yet.

"Well, she has a point there Liyah."

"I hear what y'all saying, but he's just a child. I gotta go about this the way I see fit and at this point, I'm just tryna right my wrongs." I couldn't blame him if he did want revenge. But when I looked in his eyes at that dinner table he looked like a child that needed a mother's love. Right now I was willing to step in and be that for him. Hearing the door chime I looked up to see Shawn walking in with a bouquet of red roses. My face lit up at the thoughtful gift.

"Good evening ladies," he spoke to Lou and Emi who gave him a smile and hand wave. Since the day he stopped traffic, we had spoken over the phone and via text a couple times. We were mostly catching up and getting to know each other again. It was refreshing to say the least.

"And who might you be handsome?" Lou asked before I could introduce him.

"My name is Shawn, I'm a friend of Liyah's."

"Mmhmm." She sized him up making me chuckle. I looked over just in time to see Emi with her phone out.

"What you doing Emi?"

"Oh, nothing, just recording Lou flirting with this guy like Pops ain't crazy." She held her phone at an angle. "Say what you said again Lou. This time just a little louder."

"Girl, gimmie that damn phone." Lou chased after her as she ran to the back of the shop.

"What you doing popping up on me with roses and shit like you like me?" I blushed when he kissed my cheek and placed the bouquet in front of me.

"I do like you and shit. That ain't gon' never change," he responded smoothly. Seeing the roses up close, I noticed that there were hundred-dollar bills wrapped around the petals. It was so ghetto but so sweet. I damn sure was gon' take his money, ain't no shame in my game. "You like that lil' touch I put in there huh." He smirked while patting his chest as if he was telling himself good job.

"It was a nice touch. Thank you for this. What you got going on today?"

"Just finished taking care of some business. I stopped by to see if I could have you for the rest of the day." He just didn't know how that translated in my head. "We could do what you thinking too ma. You biting that bottom lip in a way that tells me you're not thinking about food." Yep, I was definitely caught.

Shoving him, I laughed. "Stop paying attention to every little thing. I guess I can bless you with my company for today. Let me just go let my daughter and stepmom know I need them to close down the shop." Of course I put an extra switch in my walk as I walked away, as if I need to add any more bounce to this ass that shook whenever I moved.

"Hey, I'm headed out for a little bit. I'll be home a little later." Lou gave me a wink and Emi clapped her hands.

"You go 'head and get yo' groove back mama." I waved her off and went back to the front where Shawn waited patiently.

"Okay, I'm all yours." He rubbed his hands together like he had plans for me. We walked out hand in hand to his Mercedes Maybach. Yea, I still kept up with cars even while I was locked up, so I knew the good shit. Like a gentleman, he opened my door and made sure I was secure before walking over to the driver's seat. As soon as he pulled off his music came through the speakers with heavy bass. *If, only you knew, how much I do, do love you. Then you wouldn't be trippin' 'bout my niggas, no. And you wouldn't be trippin 'bout these bitches, no. You don't know, you don't know, you don't know. Baby you don't know, you don't know, you just don't know.*

I didn't know the song, but I knew Tank's sexy ass voice anywhere. I guess this was the best song for the moment. Getting comfortable in the seat, I bobbed my head to the music while Shawn whipped the car like a Nascar driver. I don't know why it made me think of Eli and how he used to drive fast as hell with me in the passenger side calm as ever. After a little drive, we arrived in front of The Alexander at Rego Park. He turned the music down low once we were parked.

"You live here?"

"Yea, I didn't wanna do the normal shit and just take you out to eat. I wanted to cook for you. You cool with that?" I nodded my head yes. I was gonna let everything happen, naturally. I had fourteen years of playing with myself. It would be nice to feel some prime wood; if you know what I mean. He was so affectionate, holding my hand as we stepped into the elevator. As we made our way into his apartment building it dawned on me that if we did go to third base tonight he'd be the second man I let penetrate me. Damn, I didn't even go through a hoe phase like most young girls did. I chuckled to myself, but loud enough for him to turn to me.

"You good?"

"Yea, just something funny I thought about." Bing! The elevator signaled that we had arrived at our stop. He let me walk in front and guided me with his hand on the small of my back. In his apartment, I nodded my head in appreciation of the décor. The 9ft ceilings and expansive windows captured the view and maximized the lighting.

"You wanna sit in the kitchen with me while I cook or put your feet up in the living room?"

"Oh, I'm gon' watch you for sure. Gotta make sure your ass ain't tryna poison me on the low," I joked seriously. You can never be too careful.

He chuckled before washing his hands. "Alexa, play R&B playlist," he called out and Mariah Carey's "We Belong Together" crooned through the speakers. While he cooked I grabbed my sketchbook from my Fendi tote bag to work on some designs. Each song that played seemed like it was having the conversation for us. We would sneak peeks at each other when certain lyrics played, speaking with our eyes. He had the house smelling amazing with the different spices that he was using. I had to stop myself from going to the pots and sneaking a taste.

As if he could hear my thoughts he came over with a spoon with sauce on it. "Here, taste this." He put the wooden spoon to my mouth and I opened my mouth to taste.

"Mmm," I moaned, loving the creamy taste and giving him a thumbs up. *It ain't no secret that I'm different since you ain't around me, that's you, you, you. Promise I won't tell nobody how you got this side of me shining through. They ain't gotta know what we do. You got the magic and I gotta have it, just for me and you, just for me and you.* This playlist had me feeling some type of way. Taking the spoon from him, I placed it on my sketchbook and leaned in and placed a french kiss on his lips.

Feeling myself get hot, I went with the feeling and climbed on the island to get closer to him. Kicking my sketchbook to the floor along with the spoon, I wrapped my arms around his neck so not to break the lock I had on his lips. Nothing felt rushed, everything felt just right in this moment. Breaking the kiss, he called out for Alexa to play August Alsina's new album. Turning off the oven, he held his hand out for mine. Without a second thought I let him walk me to his bedroom.

He held me around my waist and stared directly into my eyes. "Is it possible to still be in love with someone after so many years?" I didn't wanna answer, afraid of saying what was on my mind, so I kissed him. I kissed his head, then his nose, his cheeks, his neck, and then finally his lips. He rubbed his hands up and down my back in a sensual manner before pulling at my shirt and lifting it over my head. Stepping back, I did the honors of removing the rest of my clothes. I wasn't ashamed of my body at all. As a matter fact, I loved me so much I gave him a spin so that he could take it all in. "You about to fuck my head up."

"No baby, I'm gonna give you the answer to your question." Laying back on his bed, I spread my legs as far as they could go and played with my wet box as he undressed. His eyes watched me hungrily as I skillfully explored myself in anticipation of the dick down. "Mmmm," I moaned in ecstasy as my two fingers tapped at my g-spot. With my eyes closed, I worked myself to the point where I was ready to explode. Feeling my fingers being moved from me I opened my eyes. I watched as Shawn nastily sucked on my fingers before positioning himself in front of my pussy.

He stuck out his tongue and licked my whole pussy, making me shiver and scoot up on the bed. He grinned like he knew something I didn't. Spreading my pussy lips, he sucked on my clit using just the right amount of pressure, and that was all it took. I held the sheets as I squirted. "Arghh fuck, shit Shawn, wait." Ignoring my pleas, he sucked harder, draining me of everything I had. It'd been way too long.

"Don't tap out on me Liyah. This shit is a long time coming, you gon' take this dick." Pulling me to the edge of the bed, he twisted me in the scissor position and slowly entered me. The position was perfect, so that I could get used to his size. "Mmmhmm, this pussy tight as fuck, goddamit." He smacked my ass before giving me his full length. I rocked back and forth getting myself situated.

"I got this baby," I said with much confidence before throwing this forty-four-inch ass on him properly.

"Yea ma, throw that shit back, just like that."

"Ohhh shittt, I'ma cum." I felt myself about to release again. He grabbed hold of my waist and hit my g-spot mercilessly until we both came.

"I still love you Aaliyah Jones."

I didn't mean to spend the night, but by the time I came alive again from all that sexing it was eight am. We had done so much rolling around, we forgot all about the food from the night before. I called myself trying to sneak out of the bed with the covers still wrapped around me.

"How you gon' sneak out with my sheet and leave a nigga ass naked?" I turned to find Shawn sitting up with a hard on. "You gon' look or you gon' help me out?"

"Sorry boo, I gotta get going. You got a toothbrush I can use?"

"Yea, I put one on the sink for you last night." As I went to walk around to his side of the bed to the bathroom he smacked my ass. While taking care of my hygiene I heard his doorbell ring. I silently cursed myself for leaving my clothes on the floor by the bed. Done brushing my teeth, I backtracked to the bedroom to get dressed.

"Who you got in here that got you pulling out the good pots to cook in?" I heard a woman say as Shawn scolded her for coming in his house without taking off her shoes. See, this the kind of bullshit I didn't wanna deal with. I hoped it wasn't the chick from a couple weeks ago that he left in the car. I was sure about to go back to jail for ringing her neck if she said anything out of the way to me. I drowned

out their conversation and continued to get dressed. Using the hair tie on my wrist, I threw my hair in a ponytail and walked to the front to grab my shoes and purse.

"I know the fuck you don't got this bitch that killed our blood coming from your bedroom," TT's ghetto ass shouted. I shook my head and moved towards the island where my sketchbook still lay on the floor. I wasn't even gonna respond until she lunged at me, but Shawn grabbed her before she could actually hit me.

"Yo, chill the fuck out TT," he said, pushing her back forcefully.

"You betta listen to ya cousin because the way I'm feeling about that pussy ass move you just pulled, we can get to boxing in this bitch." I dropped my sketchbook on the counter and took a step toward her so she knew just how serious I was. Shawn made sure to stay in the middle of the two of us.

"Bitch, fuck you. You ain't 'bout to box shit. You a backstabbing ass bitch. I knew there was a reason I never liked you," she spat harshly before trying to get at me again.

"TT, get the fuck out man. This ain't the fucking hood bruh," Shawn growled, pushing her back again.

She looked at him with a hurt expression. "Really Shawn, you choosing this bitch over yo' family? Say no more." She went to leave but doubled back to threaten me. "Bitch, you gon' get yours."

"Good thing I'm always ready." Opening the door, she made sure to slam it behind her as she left. I continued to gather my belongings while Shawn watched me.

"Man, I'm sorry for that. She normally calls before she pops up." He looked stressed as he ran his hands over his face.

"No need to be sorry, that's your family. You don't have to worry about dropping me off. I'm gonna catch one of those Ubers back to the shop where my car is." I was nonchalant in my response, but inside I was pissed the fuck off.

He stopped me as I went to walk off. "Wait, come on, don't leave like this. I can drop you off Liyah, it's no problem." Stopping short, I looked in his face as tears built up in the corner of my eyes.

"I didn't mean to kill her Shawn." He didn't say anything, just pulled me into his chest and held me tight.

"I know ma, I know. I got you, I swear I do." He cupped my face in his hands and kissed my lips. Little did he know; this shit would never work.

Shawn

"I seen her with my own eyes Grams. She came out of his room looking like she had just woke up." I walked in on TT talking to Grams in her apartment. She looked shocked to see me and mad that I had walked in on her talking shit.

"Don't stop talking now. I'm here, say what you gotta say," I encouraged. She was the one cousin I couldn't stand because she was always keeping up some bullshit.

"Shawn, fuck you. As long as you fucking with the opps don't even speak to me." She rolled her eyes and I hoped that God granted my wish and made them bitches get stuck.

"Stop cussin' in my damn house like I'm not sitting right here," Grams scolded us while lighting a cigarette. "Sit down grandson, let me talk to you." Here we go with the bullshit. I sat in the fold-up chair in the corner and prepared myself. TT got up to walk out, but Grandma motioned for her to sit down.

"Grams I'm not tryna be in the room with him for too long."

"Girl, shut yo' ass up. Now listen here, I don't believe Liyah killed Erica on purpose." I sat up willing to listen now while TT sucked her teeth. "That girl loved Erica like she was her sister. Now TT, don't sit here and play dumb, acting like you didn't know Erica was sleeping with that girl's husband."

"Grams that's not the point though. She didn't have to do her like that," TT said on defense again.

"Do her like what? Whip her ass after catching her with her man? I've whipped bitches' ass for less baby. I'm not saying that I'm not hurt that my grandbaby is dead, my heart still feels the loss. What I'm saying is Liyah paid her debt to society and suffered enough. She was taken from her child as well. You ain't gotta like the girl, but know that she is gonna be out living her life."

"Exactly," I added.

"Boy shut up. I don't need no help making my point." I smiled with my hands up in mock surrender. "Yo' heart still beat for that girl after all these years. I'm gon' say this and be done with it. If you gonna pursue her, treat her right and be mindful of what she's capable of." I nodded my head in understanding. She didn't have to worry about that. I was gonna have Liyah this time around.

"I don't care what y'all say, there will never be a kumbaya moment with her and me after what she did." TT stood up and stormed out. I went to say something, but Grams stopped me.

"Let her go. She's entitled to her feelings." I did as she asked and sat back down. The last thing I wanted was to have issues with my family over me being with Liyah, but I couldn't make them accept her. "You're gonna have to protect her grandson," Grams said, pulling me from my thoughts.

"What you mean?"

"Word on the street is that Will and Pam are out for revenge. You know I never liked that bitch and her ass is slicker than a can of oil. Make sure you keep your eyes open for both you and Liyah. You know if something happens to you by her hand I'm coming out of retirement." Well that shit threw me for a loop. Will was my boy. We no longer worked closely like we used to since I had my own operation within the business, but we always saw each other in passing and it was always nothing but love.

Thanking Grams for the heads up, I got ready to leave. I needed to go holla at Will about the bug that was just put in my ear. I decided to pull up on him at his trap near the main warehouse where the product was pushed out of. On the drive there, I started to think about Liyah and how she'd been dealt a fucked-up hand. I was glad Grams was on the same page as me about the way she was being treated. After Erica had died my family was out for blood, especially her mom. She even offered me a couple bands to take Liyah out during court, knowing I was the only person that could get close to her due to our history. Of course I shut that shit down. I made it known out the gate that I held no hate in my heart for shorty, and that wasn't changing.

Arriving at the warehouse I noticed Will and Pam outside engaged in a heated argument. *Here we go with some more odd shit*, I thought to myself. What could they possibly be arguing about? I looked on as Pam flailed her hands in the air and Will swiped his hand across his face. He looked stressed as fuck. Getting out of my car, I walked over to them to see what was going on.

"Yo', what's good Shawn," Will spoke, nodding his head toward Pam whose back was facing me.

"Wassup." I dapped him up. "Everything good with y'all?" I asked once Pam turned around to face me. Her face was turned up as always.

"We good, are you good?"

"I'm great. I came here to rap with my man right here about something." I pointed to Will, who looked uncomfortable.

"Oh yea? Well, let me let you get to that," she said with an undertone that I wasn't feeling. "Will, don't forget what I said. I'll see you around Shawn." She smirked before getting in her car and racing out the parking lot. I watched her drive off before turning back to Will.

"What the fuck was that all about?"

"I don't know man. You know Pam be doing some off shit sometimes. Wassup though, what you wanted to holla at me about?" He leaned against his car, pulling a blunt from his ear and lighting it.

"You heard about Liyah being home?" I started with an easy question first.

"Yea, I heard they let the bitch out."

"Ay man, watch that shit my nigga."

"Man, you still soft on that girl dawg? Even after what she did? Man fuck her, real shit." He was passionate with the venom he was spitting. Yea, Grams was right.

"So it is true?"

"What's true nigga?"

"You on some get-back shit with Liyah." I baited him to see how much he would tell.

"Go 'head with that bullshit. If I was on some get-back, her ass would have been a distant memory soon as she came out on the other side of those steel doors when she was released," he spat venomously. If I didn't believe that Pam was in on this plan with him, I would've put his brain on the pavement right here. Although I wanted to respond with the same energy he was giving me, I knew I couldn't let on that I was on her side.

"I hear you my nigga, you and everybody else. I'm just letting you know whatever you got planned, that shit is bound to be bad for business. A war with the Joneses is not what we need right now."

"Fuck you telling me that for?"

"'Cause you the motherfucka I'm standing in front of. Plus you seem to be getting real close to Pam, so you can deliver the message. I'm not sure what she told yo' ass, but you betta stop acting off your fucking emotions about some shit that happened over a decade ago. Remember ain't no money in your feelings." Tapping his shoulder, I left him standing there. I had to get with Liyah and let her know what was going on.

I texted her letting her know I needed to holla at her in person. She hit me back immediately letting me know she'd be free later. In the meantime I decided to pull up on Eli to check in with him. Pulling up at a red light I went to turn on the radio when shots rang out. *Ra ta tat ta tat tat.* It took only a second for me to realize it was my car getting hit up. "What the fuck?!" I yelled out, hitting the gas hard to get out of the line of fire. I kept speeding until I got to my homegirl Rhonda's house on Convent Ave. Parking the car, I pulled my gun from the glove compartment and looked around for the car. Realizing it hadn't followed me, I felt a stinging sensation in my arm.

Checking myself I noticed a small hole in my elbow. Niggas had caught me slipping. Banging my good hand against the steering wheel I pulled out my phone to dial Rhonda's number. The phone immediately connected to the Bluetooth speaker and she answered on the third ring.

"You got some fucking nerve calling me. What do you want Shawn?"

"Yo, fuckk," I winced in pain as I moved my arm. "It's an emergency ma. I'm in front of your building, you home?" Sensing the urgency in my tone she changed her attitude.

"Yea, I'm home. What's wrong? What kind of emergency you talking about?"

"Come downstairs real quick man. Hurry up Rhonda, no bullshit." I disconnected the call because I felt myself getting light headed. I leaned my head against my window and breathed through the pain. It felt like eternity before she finally made it downstairs. Hearing a knock on the window I pointed the gun towards it. Seeing it was her I lowered it and unlocked the passenger side door.

"Oh shit, what the fuck. You bleeding Shawn," she said frantically. I wanted to say bitch duh but decided against it being that she was the person who was gonna help me.

"I know ma, somebody hit me up. Help a nigga out and patch..." I passed out before I could finish my sentence. I woke up to water running. Opening my eyes I shot up and went for my gun. Realizing it wasn't on me I focused my eyes on my surroundings and breathed a sigh of relief once I realized I was in Rhonda's bedroom.

"Oh, thank God you're alive," Rhonda said dramatically walking into the room in her Ethika women's sports bra and matching briefs. She looked good as fuck. I shifted in the bed to hide my hard on.

"Yea, I'm good. Thank you for patching me up." I motioned in the direction of the bandage she had wrapped around my elbow. Rhonda was a nurse at Harlem Hospital. She came in handy for things such as this.

"No problem. What the fuck happened out there today?" Her guess was as good as mine. I had no idea who'd wanna hit me up. I had no beef with nobody. I was one nigga in the game that could honestly say I had more people that loved me than hated me.

"Shorty I couldn't even tell you. This shit happened while I was sitting at a red light. I know whoever the nigga was, he better get missing asap." I was heated like a motherfucka that a nigga was bold enough to bust at me. "Aye, can you grab me my phone please? And any kind of pain meds you may have, my fucking arm is throbbing." She handed me my phone and went off to grab the meds. I checked my messages and saw that I had a message from Liyah letting me know she was free now. That was about an hour ago. Texting her back as best as I could with my good arm, I told her I'd be with her as soon as I could and that I'd had an accident. I hit send on the message and before I could put the phone back down she was FaceTiming me.

"Well damn girl, you must really be feeling a nigga," I joked once her face came into view.

"What kind of accident were you in Shawn?" she asked, concerned. I turned the camera to my arm so she could see the bandage.

"I got hit up earlier. Not even five minutes after I texted you."

"What the hell, shit, are you good? Where are you?"

"I'm straight ma. I passed out for a bit from the pain, but I'm good. I'm at my homegirl house right now, she patched me up." I turned to see Rhonda standing at the door with a scowl on her face. I went to ask her what was wrong, but her throwing the pill bottle at me threw me off. "Yo, what the fuck is wrong with you? Liyah let me hit you back." I hung up before she could respond.

"You so fucking inconsiderate and disrespectful as fuck my nigga," Rhonda said walking over and punching me in my bad arm.

"Arghhh," I gritted down on my teeth. "Are you fucking retarded girl? What the fuck is yo' problem?" My arm started to throb again. Quickly grabbing the pill bottle she threw at me, I popped it open and tossed back two pills with no water.

"Why you FaceTime a bitch while you in my house? That shit is wrong as hell." I looked at her like she was crazy.

"How is that wrong bruh? We not together. Why you tripping?"

"Don't even worry about it Shawn. Here, you're patched up and good to go." She handed me my gun from her nightstand and walked around the bed to the door.

"Look, I'll go, but tell me wassup."

"Wassup is you don't care about my feelings. You come around when you please, stick your dick down my throat, and fuck me sore but I'm the fucking homegirl! Where they do that at?" Now I was completely thrown. Rhonda and I had been fucking around for the past two years and I did consider her a homegirl. A homegirl that I'd smash every now and then. I didn't think it was a problem up until now.

"You mad at me about that? We never had a conversation about a relationship Ro. So why you coming with this shit outta nowhere, I don't understand. Right now I don't have time to talk about it. As you can see I got some shit going on, so let me get up outta here."

"Yea whateva, take yo' ass on like you always do. I'll send you a bill for my fucking services." Shaking my head, I sat up carefully and slid my sneakers on. Grabbing my piece and my phone I got up outta there. While in the elevator I called Liyah to see if she could pick me up and reached out to one of my workers to come get my car. I couldn't ride around in it in that condition. Liyah agreed to scoop me so I waited in my car on the passenger side.

I sat there replaying the incident over in my head to try to figure out if I saw anything out of the ordinary while driving. The only thing that stuck out to me was the fact that I had got hit up after I left Will. I didn't even get a chance to see the fucking driver, so right now I had nothing to go on. I would be putting some ears to the streets though, believe that. Seeing a Range Rover Coupe with tinted windows pull up, I put my gun at my side waiting for the window to roll down. Aaliyah's face became clear as the window rolled down partially.

"You need help getting in?" she asked in a warm voice.

"Nah, I'm good." Taking the spare key from under the mat I placed it on the seat before exiting and getting in the passenger side of her car. "Thanks for coming. I'm waiting on my mans to come and pick this up." I kissed her cheek making her smile.

"No worries, I got you. Somebody is pulling up behind me to tow your car to my dad's shop. We can get it cleaned up there." On cue, a tow truck pulled up behind us and did its thing lifting my car onto the flat bed. *Now that's what I'm talking about.* I texted my mans to tell him I was good and we drove off. I had definitely just found my Bonnie.

Pam

"Tell me something good," I spoke into the phone while steering my car into the parking lot of Garden State Mall.

"I did what you asked, but I don't know if he got hit or not. He sped off," Will replied while inhaling. My hands gripped the steering wheel tightly as I cracked my neck. This fucking guy couldn't seem to do anything right and at this point, this shit was not going the way I planned.

"You know what Will, I'm starting to feel like you're not the man for the job. I gave you two simple tasks and you failed both. Clearly you're not cut out for this grown man shit." I had to light a fire under his ass. I hoped that by insulting him it would work.

"Yo', you might be the boss and all that, but you ain't the one out here bussin' your gun, I am. And I don't care what you say, you don't have anyone else that's as invested in this shit like I am. Let's be clear, I'm doing this shit on the strength of Erica. I loved her in spite of all we went through together. Why the fuck we tryna hit Shawn anyway?"

"He chose his side and it wasn't ours. Something gotta give because we can't keep fucking missing. The city is not big enough for me and Aaliyah to live in together without her paying handsomely. Between you and Eli, this shit ain't getting done as fast as I need it to. I gotta make a move that I'm sure will shake things up a bit. Standby, I'll call you in a couple days." Clicking the red phone button on my steering wheel I disconnected the call and dialed another number.

"Pam," the raspy voice came through with a cough.

"I'm calling in that favor. This is big, so I don't need no fuck ups."

"Whatever you need Queen." *That's what I like to hear.*

"I need the girl."

"It's done." Nothing else needed to be said. I hung up the phone and my face turned into a sinister smile. In order to get things done, you gotta do it yourself.

Weeks later, I sat at a candlelight dinner with Tim at Clyde Frazier's. We were celebrating his new position at work. Tonight I put all of my planning to the back burner and just focused on my man. I had even gon' as far as to book us a hotel so I could celebrate him the right way.

"I'm so proud of you babe. You deserve the position you've worked so hard for."

"Thank you love. It's been a long road but it worked out in the end. I appreciate you for taking me out tonight. I'm so stuffed I don't think I can eat anymore."

"Oh, I'm sure you can find room for something else to snack on." I winked, making him chuckle.

"That's a no brainer woman. Let me go to the men's room, grab the check so we can get outta here." He stood and kissed my lips before walking away. I motioned for the waitress so she could bring the check. Busy in my phone, when the check was placed on the table I said thank you without looking up.

"Did Black not teach you anything about being aware of your surroundings?" My head shot up at the mention of my ex-husband. I looked directly into the irises of Iman Jones. He sat cooly in Tim's chair in a suit that fit his body so well. I wasn't sure what he was doing these days, but he was aging well.

"Black couldn't have taught me anything even if I gave him the manual. To what do I owe the pop up?" I asked placing my phone on the table and my hand on my purse where my gun was. He smirked deviously watching my every move.

"There was an incident a couple months ago and the car used in that incident was traced back to one of your associates. Normally I wouldn't bother with petty things such as this, but this particular incident involved my family directly. Would you happen to know anything about it?"

"You have to be a little more specific Iman." I knew he was referring to the shooting at the jail and I was silently cursing myself for not ensuring none of this shit came back to me. He sat up in the seat and stared blankly.

"You see, I've been in this game for a long time, you know that. And I know enough to know that you've been plotting against my daughter since the judge banged that gavel fourteen years ago. I can't imagine what it's like to lose a child, and I don't plan on finding out. Remember you have people close to you as well." He stood and I pulled my gun from my purse, placing it on my lap. "Give Tim my best on the promotion." Leaning in, he kissed my forehead and I felt a chill go down my spine.

I sat with my hand gripped tightly around my Ruger and my leg bouncing up and down. This visit just told me that Iman had been following me just as close as I'd been following his daughter. Quickly grabbing my phone, I called Eli to check on him and make sure he was good. He assured me that he was fine. Tim came back to the table after being gone for close to five minutes.

"All good babe? Why your leg jumping?"

"I'm good. Come on, let's get outta here." I dropped a few hundred dollars on the table and walked out in front of him to the car. He had to practically skip to keep up with my pace.

"Whoa, whoa, slow down Pam." I ignored him, not stopping until I got into the car. "What the hell is going on?" he asked, clearly confused and annoyed.

"I'm good babe, I promise. I just wanna get home." Staring at me suspiciously, he said nothing. Opening my phone I sent a text to the number I called earlier.

Me: *Do it now*

Unknown: *Got u.*

If Iman thought he was going to come and threaten me like I was some punk ass bitch, he had another thing coming. Fuck him and anyone else with the last name Jones; I had something for they ass. Tim hopped out the car before I did once we pulled up at my apartment. I had completely forgot about this night being about him. Little did he know, I had just saved his life; he'd thank me later.

Once in the house I went straight to Eli's room to check on him. Knocking on the door, he called out for me to come in. Walking in the room I headed straight toward him and hugged him tightly. He looked at me strange but allowed me to embrace him. Eli was all I had left of my daughter and after Iman popped up on me, I decided that I couldn't keep putting him in the middle of this shit I had going on. He was young and the last thing I should've been burdening him with was revenge.

"Listen grandson, as of tonight, I no longer want you around Emi or Aaliyah. Some shit is about to go down and I would die if you were caught in the crossfire." He went to protest, but I stopped him. "It's not up for discussion Elijah. I was wrong for getting you in this shit in the first place. Tonight put some things in perspective. Gma got this." I kissed his forehead and left his room, closing the door behind. me. My phone vibrated in my hand, and I looked to see a text along with an image. Opening the text there was a message from unknown and a picture of a figure seated with duct tape over their eyes. Got em'.

I went into my master bath to get my thoughts together. I had just made a chess move and I needed to make sure I had all my ducks in a row. This was sure to get Aaliyah to come to me. Let the games officially began.

Emery

Tonight Dre and I had decided to go out to Dave & Buster's to hang out. I wanted to bring Porscha, but he said his cousin had gon' out of town with his family this weekend, so he didn't want Porscha feeling like the third wheel. Agreeing, I opted out of calling her. Deciding to drive my car in case I wanted to dip out, I met him at the Dave & Busters at the Palisades Mall in Westchester. It was around six when I pulled into the packed parking lot. Texting my mom to let her know I had arrived, I texted Dre next. After he let me know he was already in the mall I headed in to meet him.

Stepping out of my car I had an eerie feeling as I walked through the parking lot to the front door. Making sure my knife was secure in my See by Chloe crossbody bag I made it inside safely. Trying my best to shake the feeling, I made my way to the Dave & Buster's entrance. Seeing Dre at the front I walked over to him.

"Wassup shorty." He hugged me and kissed my cheek. "I already paid so we can just go right in, you good?" he asked, catching me looking around.

"Yea, I'm straight. Come on, let's go inside." He took my hand in his and led the way. The night ended up being fun once I put that eerie feeling to the back of my mind.

"I'm happy I was able to make you smile tonight," Dre said once we sat down to eat.

"Me too, I had sworn in the car that if you fucked up in any way I was leaving yo' ass right in this place by yourself." I chuckled and he joined me.

"Damn, you cold blooded." We ate and played some more games before deciding to wrap everything up. I gotta admit I was surprised that I enjoyed myself so much. Dre kept his hands to himself and had me dying laughing the entire time. He walked me to my car and all of a sudden that eerie feeling came back again, but this time it was stronger than before. Before I could address it a cloth was put over my face and I fell out.

When I came to, I was sitting up in what felt like a chair with my hands tied behind my back and tape around my eyes. I didn't know where I was or what was going on, but I knew it wasn't good. Using my senses, I sniffed the air and was able to smell an Air Wick plug which led me to believe I was in someone's house. I didn't panic so I also knew I wasn't in a small space. Just before I went to yell out I heard a conversation happening. The people weren't in the room with me because they didn't sound close, but they seemed close enough where I could hear what they were saying.

"Yo, she's here. I did what you asked, now y'all gotta get somebody to watch her. I can't sit in here with her like that. This shit is fucked up man."

"You gon' sit in there for as long as I need yo' ass to. Yo' daddy owe me this favor, so sit yo' ass down, feed her every now and then, and keep her hydrated until I call you back with further instructions."

"*Fuckkkkkk!*" I heard Dre yell out, and a shattering noise followed. Now I was pissed. This pussy really helped somebody fucking kidnap me. Oh my fucking god, I was lured to Dave & Buster's. This nigga really played me. Hearing the door open, he walked down five steps, I counted in my head.

"Take this tape off my eyes, pussy. Let me look in your face," I taunted him, trying to get in his head. Silence. He didn't say anything, but I could tell he was still there by his breathing. Dre was nervous and had no clue what he had gotten himself into. I planned on using that to my advantage. "Dre, why would you do this to me? What is it that you want?" Again, he remained silent. I started to sniffle as if I was crying. That got him to move closer to me. Bingo!

"Fuck man, Emery what the fuck are you mixed up in?" he cursed as if he was the one in distress. I hung my head and started to sniffle louder. Feeling the tape being removed from my eyes gently, I knew I had him. I looked up at him with tears in my eyes.

"What's going on Dre? Please, just let me go." He ran his hand down his face and let out a long sigh before stepping back.

"I don't know what's going on. My pops hit me up a couple weeks back telling me he owed some lady a favor and that he needed my help. He was told I needed to kidnap a girl and hold her until I was given further instructions. That girl just happened to be you."

"What? But your father doesn't even know me and what lady are you talking about?" I kept my voice as even as I could. I really wanted to say fuck you and yo' punk ass daddy and then threaten him with the consequences of his actions, but he'd feel them soon enough.

"Some woman named Pam Black. She seems to have it out for your whole family. She had seen us that day at the movies and I guess she put two and two together." Damn, Eli's grandmother was behind this whole shit. The world was too damn small.

"Dre, I really need you to let me go. If my mom and pop find out you were behind this, which they will, my pop will kill every single person in your family including the family dog," I warned.

"I wish I could let you go, but I can't. I'm not gonna put the tape around your eyes, but if you start screaming or doing anything crazy I will, and I'll have to duct tape your mouth." I had nothing to say. I had given him a way out of this and he didn't take it. I would be quiet from now on and wait for my family to come for me.

It had been two days since I'd been in this room and no one had come for me yet. I wasn't discouraged though. My phone had a gps tracking device on it so I'm almost sure my mom had tracked it like I taught her before it died. Hearing the door creak open, two people descended the steps that I hadn't seen since I'd been locked up in here. The man looked shocked to see me tied up and the woman who I'd come to know as Pam Black, Eli's grandmother, had a stern face.

"Hello Emery." It took everything in me not to spit in her face. "I don't wanna hurt you. I actually want your mom to replace you in that chair you're in."

"Girl, fuck you. The fact that you doing all this for your slutty ass daughter is a joke." WHAP! She slapped me so hard my head jerked back and blood trickled down the side of my mouth. The guy said nothing, just sat in a chair in the corner.

"Now you listen here you little bitch, you're gonna watch the way you speak to me. I'm not beneath killing a kid. Especially in the mood I'm in. Here, take this phone and call your mother." She handed me my halfway charged iPhone XR for me to dial my mom. Using my facial expression, I did as she requested. My mother picked up on the first ring like I knew she would, and I put her on speaker phone.

"Emi Ice," she spoke in a calm tone. Well to an outsider it may have seemed calm, but to someone who knew her it was everything but.

"Yea Ma, it's me." Pam snatched the phone from my hand before I could say anything else.

"Aaliyah, do you love your daughter?"

"As much if not more than you loved yours," she responded.

"Would you trade your life for hers?"

"In a heartbeat."

"Well I'd like to test that theory. I'm gonna text you the address to where we are and I want you in exchange for her. This is not a game

I'm playing here. You owe me for what you did and somebody gotta pay in blood. Whether it be you or her is your choice."

"Oh bitch, I'm coming. Before I go, I have someone that wants to speak to you."

"Gma, I'm good," I heard Eli's voice and thought to myself, *my mom is a bad bitch*. I looked on as Pam's eyes got wide and she tried her best to control her emotions.

"You bitch, you lay a finger on his head and I'll slit her fucking throat from ear to ear." She looked at me when she said it, hoping to evoke some fear in me. I was a Jones though; I was trained for things such as this. She hung up my phone and threw it to the ground. Good thing I had my otter box case so it didn't shatter when it landed at my feet.

"Ain't no fun when the rabbit got the gun," I taunted. She nodded to the guy who sat in the corner before turning to walk away. The guy walked in front of me and bent down so that we were eye level.

"Lil' mama, this kidnapping shit wasn't Dre's idea nor mine. All we want is your mama for real. Watch what you say around Pam because you're expendable to her." I didn't know who the fuck this man thought he was, but we were a little past the fake good guy phase.

"Sir, please get the fuck outta my face before I spit on your ass." I knew that was the most vulgar thing you could do to a person and how I was feeling, I was ready to do just that. Before I knew it, he punched me right in between my eyes. "Arghhh," I screamed out in intense pain. My head fell from feeling dizzy.

"I bet yo' ass will stop talking now," he said, casually strolling away. At that point I said a quick prayer up to God to forgive me for my sins. I knew that out of the four of us, I was the only one leaving out alive. Hours had gone by and my mom had yet to arrive, but I didn't lose hope. I tried to sleep as much as I could to make the time go by faster. That worked up until the door opened again. I lifted my head, in pain, to see who it was. Seeing Dre again I sucked my teeth. He had a bag from Chipotle and that shit smelled good as fuck. I wanted to refuse the food but I knew I needed all the strength I could get.

"Hey, I brought you some food and water." He handed me the bag along with a bottle of Smart water. I looked at him like he was stupid.

"They really picked you to kidnap me bruh? Like really, did you forget that my hands were tied dummy?" I shook my head wondering what I saw in his dumbass. "You plan on untying me or you gonna feed me?"

"I'll feed you." He pulled out a chicken burrito. Thank God I wasn't allergic to anything because I went to town as soon as he put the thing to my mouth. "Damn, you was hungry."

"Shut up, and just make sure ya hand don't touch my food," I said with my mouth full. "Water please." He put the bottle to my lips and I damn near drank the whole thing.

"What the fuck happened to ya eyes?" he asked like he really cared. This dude was a real Denzel Washington.

"Oh, you skipped kidnapping 101 huh? Usually when you're kidnapped they beat yo' ass for talking shit. You can go now, I'm done." I tilted my head back on the chair and closed my eyes again. I heard him get up and start to walk away.

"I'm really sorry about this shit E." Sorry wasn't gon' cut it, the damage was already done.

Elijah

For the past few weeks, I had taken a step back from Aaliyah being that Gma basically banned me from being around her. I hadn't been privy to any info regarding taking her out. In fact, Gma had been real secretive and barely even talked business around me. I was home alone again tonight which wasn't uncommon. My phone vibrated and I looked over to see that it was Shawn texting me. Cuzzo: *Wassup lil' man. Come downstairs real quick so we can talk.* I went to look out the window and sure enough, his truck was parked in front of the building.

Grabbing my keys, I slipped on a pair of Nikes and texted him that I was on my way down. Once I made it downstairs I dapped him up and got into the passenger seat. I noticed his arm was in a sling so I pointed it out.

"The hell happened to ya arm cuzzo?" He casually glanced at it before responding.

"Ain't shit that a real nigga can't handle. Wassup witchu?"

"Nothing much, was upstairs watching tv. What is it you wanna chop it up about?" He took his keys out of the ignition and straightened his seat.

"You know anything about that failed hit that happened the day Aaliyah was released from jail?" I held his gaze, void of emotion, knowing he was looking for some type of reaction.

"Nope."

"You sure about that?" I nodded my head yes. "Aight Eli, I already know you not keeping it one hunnit with me. I'm only asking you to protect you man. Aaliyah's pops already done put two and two together so he already know ya grandmother had something to do with the hit. You young and you don't need to be caught up in this bullshit."

"Man, why you rallying so hard for the other side after what she did to yo' peoples? That shit suspect as hell." I had to say something because he was acting more loyal to them than us.

"This shit ain't about rallying for the other side. This about life and death lil' nigga. And ya grandmother sending you on that fucking dummy mission signed your death certificate. You don't think Aaliyah been on to you the day you went to that penthouse to meet with her?! Use yo' fucking brain."

"I'm smarter than you think. I've watched my gma cry her eyes out for as long as I remember behind my mama's death. You know who's responsible for that pain, Aaliyah. She killed my mother in a jealous rage with no regard for me!" I hit my chest to get my point across about how fucked up I was behind it.

"All that shit you just spilled out is straight from your grandmother telling you HER version of the story. No matter how many times you're told it was an accident, you're not gonna believe it and I understand that. The last thing I wanna see is you caught..." A knock at his window cut him off. Seeing Aaliyah's face come into view, she motioned for him to roll the window down.

"You"—she pointed to me—"step out of the car please." I looked at her like she was crazy. Although she seemed calm, the look on her face said she wasn't fucking around.

"What's going on ma?" Shawn asked.

"I haven't seen my daughter in forty-eight hours. I have no enemies outside of your family. He's coming with me and will be with me until I find her." I had no idea about Emi being kidnapped. I didn't even know that there was a plan to have her involved in this capacity. I guess I took too long to move because before I could say anything the door was being opened and I was snatched out by some buff nigga.

"Aye, watch how you fucking handle my cuz my nigga!" I heard Shawn yell out as he went to open the door on his side. I watched Aaliyah pull a gun from behind her back and hit him upside the head with it.

"Shawn! Get the fuck off me," I barked, tryna fight the guy off me before being thrown in the backseat. "Why you do that shit to him? Where you taking me?" I yelled out once she got in the driver's seat.

"Sit yo' ass back before I forget you're a child and break yo' fucking neck. I don't know why y'all came fucking with me. Clearly y'all don't know how ruthless I can get." I sat back biting my lip, trying to figure a way out of this fucked up situation.

"Yo', it's Emi's cell calling," the buff dude said as he showed her the caller ID. I listened as she put the phone on speaker. When Gma's voice came through the speaker I was stuck. She really had kidnapped Emi and left me out in the open. Aaliyah handed me the phone after mentioning she'd be there for the exchange.

"Let her know that you're good," she said covering the phone.

"I'm good Gma." She snatched the phone from me and I heard Gma shouting threats before hanging up. We drove to a house where she let the guy out and told me to get in the front seat. I couldn't comprehend why she would let me out the car. That only meant one thing, her intentions weren't to kill me. At least not now.

"Do you know what's at this address?" She showed me a text from Emi's phone with an address.

"No." We rode in complete silence to the address, no music or anything. I kept sneaking peeks at her face and she was still calm. "You real calm for someone whose daughter was kidnapped and who could die today."

"You're all your grandmother has that means something to her. Trust me, she'd wanna see you before she makes any further stupid decisions. Plus I already have people sitting outside this house we're on the way to. I just wanted to know if you were lying about not knowing anything."

"And if I was?" I challenged.

"You would've had a closed casket from the bullet I would've put in your face. Your grandmother is crazy, but I'ma geek about mine. We're here." She had me so stuck I didn't notice the car had stopped. Again I was yanked from the car, but by an older guy.

"You sure you don't want me to go in there with you babygirl?" I looked between the two of them and noticed the resemblance.

"No Daddy, I got this. Do me a favor though. Have someone go by and check on Shawn. I had to knock him out before we got here." He nodded his head and pulled me by my collar to a nearby awaiting car. "Dad," she called out to him.

"I know, don't kill him. Go get my granddaughter Aaliyah." He waved her off and pushed me into the passenger seat of the car.

"Why y'all not tying me up or anything?" I finally asked the question that had been burning in my head.

"Why haven't you tried to get away?" he retorted. I didn't have a comeback because I honestly didn't know why I didn't try to get away.

"You think she's gonna kill my grandma?" I wasn't prepared for the answer he gave.

"Yes, but she'll make it quick." I felt my heartbeat speed up at the thought of my gma dying. She was the only close family I had besides Shawn. The other side of my mom's family, she barely let me be around.

"My daughter really has a soft spot for you, you know? Despite what went down with your mother," he assured me. I scoffed at the bullshit that was coming from his lips, but it did make me think. These past weeks that I'd been around Aaliyah she knew that my intentions weren't pure but she allowed me in her space anyway. Every time I mentioned my mother I noticed she would get this sad look in her eyes. A look of regret, like the guilt of what she had done was still eating at her till this day. I had to want her dead though. I had to avenge my mother for the sake of my grandmother, right?

"What kind of person would I be if I didn't want revenge for my mother?"

"You'd be a person that was living instead of existing. You've been walking around with hate in your heart for my daughter that wasn't yours to begin with. You didn't know the full story. You knew what you were told and that created that monster within you."

"Does it really matter whether it was an accident or not though? My mother is fucking dead."

I watched him light a cigar and take one puff before responding, "Is she?"

Will

"I'm not doing this shit no more man. This shit crazy," Dre said as he came back up with the rest of the food that Emery didn't eat. He had been saying that same line for the past two days, knowing there was no way out this shit. His pops had made a deal with Pam and there was no backing out of that until the task was completed.

"Lil' nigga, go take a walk or something. I'll cover for you." He looked like he was about to lose it and I couldn't have that on my watch. Especially while I was too busy tryna keep from losing it myself. Ever since I came to Pam about Aaliyah being released and wanting to get at her, she had been on some other shit. I had to let her know on more than one occasion that I was doing this for Erica. The night I got the call about E, my heart dropped.

"Hello, this is Nurse Reed at Harlem Hospital. Do you happen to know an Erica King?"

"Yea I do, is everything okay?" I asked, now fully awake from the nap I had taken.

"Well sir, umm, I wouldn't say things are okay. Odd yes, but okay, not quite."

"Nurse, what the fuck are you tryna say?" I was getting pissed off. I hadn't spoken to Erica since the day I had left her house so I was confused as to why I'd be getting a call from the hospital.

"Sir I think it's best that we discuss this in person. Could you come down to the hospital please?" I agreed that would be best seeing as

she wasn't really telling me shit. Throwing on a pair of track pants and a hoodie, I snatched up my keys and rushed out the door. I did eighty miles-per-hour on the Westside Highway to get to the hospital. Once I made it I went to the front desk and asked for Nurse Reed who just so happened to be standing there filling out paperwork.

"Will?" she asked to verify my identity.

"Yea, that's me."

"Okay, come with me." I followed her to a hospital room where two women and a man stood outside of the door. "Will, this is our chief of surgery, our coroner, and attorney for the hospital." Everyone had a puzzled look on their faces as they shook my hand. Still, I was confused.

"Where the hell is Erica?" What was told to me next was enough to make my ass need a room next because I felt like I was in the twilight zone. "Wait, so you mean to tell me she came in here beat up and pregnant. Y'all save the baby, she flatlines, and y'all pronounce her dead. Her mama comes and sees her body in the morgue, like literally identifies the body, but she not dead. How in the fuck did that happen?"

"Well, after looking through Erica's records that we requested from her primary physician we found that Erica was diagnosed with narcolepsy catalepsy," the chief said and went on to explain the condition and how it worked.

"So I'm guessing you are here to make sure that we don't sue y'all ass for the fuck up huh?" I pointed to the attorney who was about to respond, but I cut him off. "You don't have to worry about that. I actually wanna keep this quiet. I need her to remain dead to the world. I'll handle the rest." The attorney immediately agreed, knowing if this shit got out they'd have a hard time trying to explain it.

"We put her in a medically induced coma so that she could heal from the trauma her body went through without being in severe pain. She may not remember too much once she wakes up, but we wanna keep her like that for at least a month." I agreed with the nurse and went in to see her. She looked like she was in a peaceful sleep. The bruises were extensive, but I knew she'd heal.

"E baby, I know you can hear me, it's Will. I'm here ma. You just rest up."

She remained in that condition for two months. Once she was taken out of the coma, she didn't know who I was nor why she was in the hospital. When she was released, we drove to Florida where I had a house on the beach that had been left to me by my parents when they passed. It took about a year of hard work for her to regain most of her memory. She hated the fact that she couldn't contact her mother or Eli, but I let her know it was for the best. I stressed the importance of her being dead so that Aaliyah would remain in jail. Once word got out that she was being released, she was itching to get to her.

Fast forward to now, she had been aware of every move that I made during operation "Get Back." Between having to fight with her about why she couldn't make an appearance and battling with her mother about how she wanted to handle things, I was going crazy. Everything had really gon' left once she had me hit Shawn up. That was my man fifty grand and even though he was still very much in love with Aaliyah, I knew he didn't have no ill intentions towards me or Pam. He just couldn't help who he loved. What Pam didn't know was that I missed on purpose. My aim was immaculate on my worst day. I couldn't see myself killing my boy though.

Seeing that Dre was in his feelings, I decided to go downstairs and check on Emery myself. It was no telling what he may have done since he was feeling so bad about the situation. Making it downstairs I saw that her head was back and her eyes were closed. Moving close to her I put my finger under her nose to make sure she was still breathing.

"If ya hands didn't smell so fucking bad I would've bitten ya finger." She sat up, moving my finger from her nose as best as she could being that she couldn't use her hands. Emery may have gone down as the most difficult captive in history. She always had something smart to say and she cursed us out every chance she got. "Yes, I'm still alive. Y'all don't have to keep checking on me."

"Every time I start to feel bad for you, you open your mouth little girl. We probably would've been let you go had it not been for your fucking mouth."

"Miss me with that errand boy. I'll be out soon, you watch." Shaking my head, I left out the way I came in. She was giving me a headache. This whole situation was fucking with me. Fishing my vibrating phone from my pocket, I looked down at the caller ID and threw my head back in frustration.

"Yea?" I answered.

"What's going on?" Erica asked on the other end.

"Same shit that was going on when you called me an hour ago E."

"Why y'all don't just let her go? And go at Aaliyah's ass straight up instead of sneaking like some fucking cowards. This bitch done been out of jail living her best life all this time. She done had some dick, family moments and a whole business that's booming." She pointed out all the stuff I told her.

"Yo, you and ya mama really irking me with the shit y'all think should be done, but neither of y'all are making no plays." They always had ideas, but no real execution. Kidnapping Emery was the first thing Pam had managed to actually do.

"Whatever Will, it's clear that when you want something done you have to do it yourself. Where's my mama anyway?"

"What you mean? Do what yourself? Where yo' ass at Erica?"

"I'm where I'm at." I heard the dial tone after that. This had been an ongoing thing with her and I ever since I decided to stay in New York for a while to get this Aaliyah situation taken care of. She complained that things weren't moving fast enough and a whole bunch of other shit that I ignored. At this point, I was ready to go downstairs and let the little bitch go out of spite.

"Trouble in paradise?" I looked up to see Aaliyah with a Beretta M9 pointed at me. I put my hands up and silently cursed myself, wondering how much of the conversation she heard. She walked closer and placed the gun to my forehead. I peeked around her hoping that Dre would come in and off this bitch.

"If you looking for your boy he ain't coming. Give me your phone and tell me where my daughter is."

"I ain't telling you shit!" I spat, not easily scared.

She shrugged her shoulders. "Suit yourself." She pulled a knife from her pocket and stabbed me in both of my kneecaps. Snatching my phone from my hand, she shoved it in her pocket.

"Arghhh, arghhh!" I yelled out before biting down on my lip.

"You sure you don't wanna tell me?" she asked again. This bitch was really sick. I looked up to see that her eyes had gone dark like E explained when she blacked out on her. I couldn't answer with all the pain that I was in. I pointed towards the door where Emery was being held. "Thank ya kindly. Don't go nowhere, okay?" As if stabbing me wasn't enough, she punched me in the head so hard I blacked out.

Aaliyah

The night Emery had left out for her date with her little boo I had no reason to believe that she wasn't coming home. But that's exactly what happened. I called her phone several times once midnight hit, it would ring, and then go to voicemail. That went on for a couple hours before it went straight to voicemail, meaning the phone had been turned off. I called her friend Porscha to get the number to the boy Emi had gone out with. She gave me the number with no hesitation. I called and got no answer from him either.

Immediately turning off Aaliyah, I became that bitch that nobody wanted to see. My eyes became dark and I got off the bed prepared to go to war about my seed. Still a beast with computers, I was able to search the number I had for Dre and get an address. It wasn't even thirty minutes before I was at his door. An older guy answered licking his lips as he eye fucked me.

Little did he know, I'd be the last image he had before it was lights out for his ass. He let me know that he was indeed the father of Dre. Of course, like the tough guy he made himself out to be, he kept silent about knowing Pam. That lasted all of five minutes before I took out my 9mm and shot him in the kneecap.

"Now that I have your attention sir, call your fucking son and get an address on where my fucking child is being held." I threw the phone that was sitting on the arm of his couch at him. Listening as he made the call, I tapped my foot impatiently. When he hung up, he handed me the phone and I took a picture of the address with my own. Cracking his screen, I placed it in my pocket to get rid of later.

He went to say something, but a bullet to the head silenced any other conversation he may have had. Leaving the house, I texted my dad to let him know I made a mess along with the address to where Emi was so he could meet me. He texted me back letting me know that he knew where I was and Brandon would be outside. When I made it back to my car Brandon was seated in the passenger side of my truck. He gave me a head nod and I pulled off.

The next stop was Eli's house. I hated to have to use him, but I was going to war behind Emery Iceland King. That meant anybody could get it, including Shawn. When I pulled up and noticed Eli in his car, I was hoping he wasn't down with the conspiracy to kidnap my child. Erring on the side of caution, I didn't hesitate to knock him out once Eli was out of the car. Comparing the address Dre's dad gave with the one Pam had sent, I was headed in that direction. I said a quick prayer to God to protect my daughter until I got there.

Everyone involved in the kidnapping of Emery was going to pay severely. The GPS let me know we had arrived. Seeing my dad's car I immediately handed Eli off to him. I made it perfectly clear to him what not to do. Screwing the silencer onto my gun I made my way to the front door. Before I could open it I heard someone from the side of the house.

"Fuck," the person whispered loud enough for me to hear. With the speed of a cheetah I spun around and let off a shot that landed in the middle of the person's forehead. I didn't stick around to see the body drop. Keeping on task I turned the knob, careful not to make noise as I opened the door. Before I could fully get in, a conversation stopped me in my tracks. I listened intently and my mouth dropped open. Erica had been alive this whole time and the only person who seemed to know was Will. How they were able to pull that shit off was mindblowing to me. Now I was even more pissed.

"Trouble in paradise?" I asked, making myself known. Will was caught and he knew he was fucked. He tried to tough guy talk me like Dre's dad, but that ended fast. Producing another knife from my body, I stabbed him in both kneecaps. That got him to point in the direction of a door where Emi was being held. All it took was a little persuading to get what you wanted. I teased him about not going anywhere before making it to the door.

"Emery," I called out as I opened the wooden door and descended the steps. There was no response, but something told me she was down there, so I continued to walk. The sight of my baby slumped over in a wooden chair was enough to make me scream out in anguish. Instead, I bit down hard on my bottom lip to contain myself. "Emi, baby, it's Mommy. I'm here baby."

"Ma," she spoke in a faint voice. "I knew you were coming." I hurriedly untied her and stifled a scream after seeing how the rope had torn into her skin from being tied so tight. Murder was on my mind but I had to get my daughter out of here safely. Once she was fully untied, we made our way towards the steps.

Before we could reach the first step, the door opened. "Nice of you to join us Aaliyah." I bit the side of my mouth to keep from going ballistic. Again, the plan was to get out of here safely. I'm sure my dad had seen Pam come in so I played it cool. Walking backward, I sat Emi back in the chair. "I figured you'd try to leave before I got here. Now look at you, the tough ass bitch standing on the other side of the gun."

"Pam, spare me the theatrics and tell me what the fuck you want." I wasn't interested in the whole movie scene showdown shit she was on.

She walked closed to me and put the gun to my head. "Bitch, I want my fucking daughter back. Can you give me that? No, so I'll take your life instead." I kept my eyes trained on her waiting for her to pull the trigger, but it didn't happen.

"So you wanna kill me because of what happened to Erica, I get that.

But have you ever stopped to think about how we got here?" I wanted her to be distracted, so that when I struck she'd be off her game.

"It doesn't fucking matter. She was your best friend Aaliyah!"

I was so fed up with these motherfuckas acting like this bitch was a saint. "And he was my fucking husband! She fucked him and had a whole fucking child. Y'all seem to forget that important piece. So if you wanna shoot me bitch, shoot me. You just better make sure you don't miss," I gritted.

She cocked her head to the side and stared with the gun still pointed at me. "Oh no, my dear. I know that's what you're expecting. The real reason I called you here was so that you could experience the same pain as me. Only you're going to watch me kill your daughter." Just as she went to point her gun at Emi, I pulled my knife and stabbed her in the stomach, making her drop the gun.

"Not today bitch." I watched her gasp before falling. Pulling the knife from her body, some of the blood hit my clothes. "And for the record, your daughter just may be alive, too bad you won't be able to live to find out." Seeing her eyes glaze over, I used her shirt to wipe the blood off my knife before placing it back in my hoodie, and grabbed Emi. This time we were able to fully make it up the stairs. Kicking open the door, I noticed Will had a bullet in his head. Not bothering to stop I helped my baby to my dad's car and placed her in the backseat.

"Oh shit," Eli whispered, noticing a bruised Emi. My dad didn't say anything. He shook his head and started his car.

"Doc is at the house. Let's get my grandbaby home," he said, his voice menacing.

"You gotta handle this Daddy. I need you to get me an address on this number and charter me a plane." I handed him the phone I picked up off of Will and went to the last call on his recent call list. Taking the number, I knew he'd memorized it with his photographic memory. "Mommy loves you Emi, you're gonna be okay baby, I promise. Let's go Eli." He looked back and forth between me and my dad and then back at Emi before complying with my request. I held him by his shoulder to ensure he wouldn't run and got into the driver's seat once he secured himself in the passenger's. Watching as my dad pulled off, my phone buzzed. Opening it, there was a message with a Florida address.

"I saw my grandmother go into that house. Is she dead?"

"Yes," I answered, void of any emotion. From the corner of my eye I saw his fist balled so tightly his knuckles became almost white.

"Where are you taking me?"

"To your mother."

"My mother's dead," he spat still not facing me.

"I thought so too up until I heard Will talking to her." He whipped his head in my direction. "I can show you better than I can tell you."

I didn't know what to expect once we reached Florida and headed to the address my dad sent me. The fact that Erica may have been alive this whole time was fucking with me. Why would she leave her mother to raise her son? Did she remain in the shadows all these years to ensure I'd remain locked up? These were some of the questions I had. I could only imagine what Eli was thinking. He had been quiet the entire plane and Uber ride. We pulled into a quiet cul de sac in Palm Springs, FL and I mentally prepared myself for what was sure to come. If I had to put Erica to sleep to ensure my safety as well as my daughter's, I was prepared to do that, permanently.

"We're here. Come on, let's get out," I said to a zoned-out Eli. Hesitantly, he got out and so did I. The house looked like it was built for a family. The grass was well manicured and there was even a little garden on the side of the house from what I could see. Checking to ensure my knife was secure as well as my gun that was tucked away in my joggers, I was ready to get this shit over with. "Go 'head and knock."

"And how do I know that once we get in this house you won't kill me too?"

"You don't. We're here for answers, how this is gonna turn out in the end is solely based on her." It may not have been the answer he was looking for, but it was the answer I had. I couldn't make any promises of the events to come. One thing I could guarantee was the fact that I would be coming out of the house alive. He knocked like I instructed and we waited. Time had stood still for all of a few seconds. I purposely stood behind him so that she wouldn't see me. When the door finally opened, I drew a blank.

Erica

I could feel someone poking and prodding at me, but I couldn't understand why I couldn't move. Why was it so cold in this damn room? My eyes felt so heavy, where was I? I felt a cool, sharp object on my stomach and whatever it was, I knew that it shouldn't have been on my skin. "Now it's time to cut," I heard someone say. Cut? Who was getting cut? Oh hell no. I fought through whatever state I was in and opened my eyes. A guy was standing over me in scrubs, his face became white as a ghost before he ran away. What the fuck was going on? That was fourteen years ago when I had risen from the dead; literally.

Here I was, alive and kicking after almost dying at the hands of my own best friend. I really thought I was a goner on the night she caught Eli and I together. I never thought in a million years that we'd get to where we were now. Aaliyah had caused my family a lot of pain and there was no coming back from that. While her family was able to see her on weekend visits, my family mourned me.

After hanging up with Will I was pissed the fuck off. He had yet to complete the task of killing her and that shit was bothering me something crazy. It's like she always found a way to come out on top. At this point I was ready to come out of the shadows and kill the bitch myself. For fourteen years I plotted on different ways that Will could kill her. I kept track of her through Will's cousin who worked as a C.O. at Bedford Hills where Aaliyah was locked up.

I even had Will offer her money to poison Liyah, but she turned him down. The bitch acted like her benefits were so good at the jail, pussy hoe. Every day that I sat in this house and thought back on the events that led me here, I wanted to make her suffer. I had left my son with my mom at the direction of Will. Although I had lost my memory I was aware that I had given birth to a baby boy. That shit broke my heart to have to basically give him up.

After going through that whole stint in the hospital, Will had told me how I had come back from the dead. This shit was really something out of a movie. The pills that I took daily for this narcolepsy shit I was diagnosed with were a daily reminder of the events that had me in hiding. Well that and that scar on my thigh from where Liyah had shot me. The first year in Florida was hard on me as I struggled to remember certain stuff. For a while I didn't even know who Will was, but he had given me my space to figure it out.

I may be pissed with him at the moment, but I'm forever grateful for him nursing me back to one hundred percent. I still had flashbacks every now and then to the night Liyah had killed the love of my life and almost killed me. Yes, I said the love of my life. Meko may have been her husband, but he was just as much mine as he was hers. The times we spent together were special to me and I was happy that I was able to hold onto those memories at least.

Once I fully gained my memory back, Will begged me to go to therapy to sort out the feelings I had for Meko. He claimed it wasn't healthy that I still referred to him as the love of my life when in fact he was Aaliyah's husband. He didn't understand what Meko and I shared and neither did that fucking therapist he hired that diagnosed me with a bipolar disorder. Everybody had an opinion on why sleeping with a married man, my best friend's husband at that, was so wrong. They didn't know what they were talking about. The heart wants what the heart wants, and my love for him produced a beautiful child.

Plenty of nights I'd cried myself to sleep thinking about what my life could've been had we not been caught. My son was growing up without me and all I had was pictures. I had missed his first steps, first words, and first days of school. Aaliyah owed me her life and I wanted it in blood. It would have been easy for me to have Emi killed, but once you chop off the head, the body was sure to fall. I picked up my phone again to call Will and my call went straight to voicemail. That was odd; he always made sure to answer the phone whenever I called.

Deciding I was tired of waiting around, I got up to pack a small bag. I was headed back to NY. It was clear that I would have to be the one to take care of Aaliyah. I made up in my mind that I wanted my son as well. Skeptical about how the reunion would go, I was more than willing to give him time to get used to me being around. From what I was told by the weekly report I got from Will, Eli was doing well and my mom had done a good job raising him. I knew the reunion with her wouldn't be so pretty either.

As I walked stuffing items in my carry-on, my doorbell rang. I hadn't made many friends in the time I'd been here other than my next-door neighbor Brittany. She would always call before stopping by though. Figuring it was Will popping up on me, I opened the door without looking out the peephole like I normally did.

"I guess you haven't been answering your phone because you were too busy popping up on me, hu—" the rest of my sentence got stuck in my throat as I looked into the eyes of my fourteen-year-old son. It was like seeing Meko's face all over again. My hand immediately shot up to my mouth. I was trying to process the fact that he was here in front of me. "Elijah," I whispered into my hand.

"You gon' let us in or you gon' stand there and stare at the boy?" The voice I heard made me twitch. Before I could put a face to it, Aaliyah made herself known, coming up from behind him.

"Bitch, what the fuck you doing with my son?"

"Your son? Girl, your fucking jokes. You been so called dead for how long and now you wanna claim your son?" Aaliyah shot back. I stepped back to allow them entry. I didn't want my neighbors all in my business. I looked at my son who was almost taller than me and admired his looks. He was a handsome young boy. I may have been happy about our reunion, but I could tell he certainly wasn't. I watched as Liyah took a seat on the arm of my love seat as if she had been invited. I hated that bitch so much now.

"Why you leave me?" Elijah asked, snapping me out of my thoughts of killing Liyah.

"Baby boy, I didn't wanna leave you and I regret the day that I did every single day of my life. I'm so sorry that your dad or I wasn't around to give you the parents you deserved to have." When I mentioned Meko, I made sure to look in Liyah's direction. I wanted the bitch to know that even in death I still had a connection to him.

"Girl, you the only one still stuck on his dead ass. So much so that yo' ass played dead probably wishing that you could go meet him in hell," she spat venom. Having had enough of her smart comments, I lunged at her only for Eli to grab me, giving her enough time to pull out her gun. "Come on bitch, so I can make sure you meet yo' fucking maker this time." I froze in fear that she may try to hurt Eli too.

"Bitch, fuck you. You ain't shit without that gun." I was hoping she'd drop it and shoot me a fair one. I had been training mentally and physically for this day. I didn't expect for my son to be a part of it, but fuck it. Eli let me go and moved back from me.

"You don't even care about me. I actually thought that coming here I'd be able to connect with you, seeing as though you're the only family member I have left."

"Baby boy, I love you with all my heart. You don't know what she's done to our lives, it's her fault we're here. And what do you mean the only family member you have left? Your grandmother loves you."

"She's fucking dead bruh. She's dead because of you!" he yelled out, falling to his knees sobbing. Liyah immediately went to him making me lunge at her again.

"Get away from my son bitch. This shit is all your fault." I pushed her off of him, not caring that she had a gun in her hand. I went to hold Eli, but he pushed me away breaking my heart into a million pieces when he went to stand next to Liyah. "It's bad enough that you killed his dad, now my mom too and you tryna take my son from me. Were you ever my fucking friend Liyah?"

"That's the problem E, I've always been your friend. Since day one I've had your back right, wrong, or indifferent. You fucked my husband multiple times and had a fucking child like everything was all good. You are the reason for where we are now. It's about time you start admitting your faults in all this," she said with not one ounce of remorse for taking the lives of my loved ones. "Eli, go outside to the Uber please," she spoke, and I looked at him seeing who he was gonna choose. He looked back and forth between her and I before walking out.

In that moment, I was defeated. My son had made his choice and there was nothing I could do about it. I watched him walk out the door without so much as a hug. Once the door was closed, the gun I had tucked, I pointed directly at her. I would never let this bitch have one up on me ever again.

"Is this what you wanted, to have my son? My life just wasn't enough huh? You always have to be on the winning side while I'm always left with the short end of the stick."

"What the hell are you talking about Erica? Winning side? I never knew we were in competition." She tried to play dumb like I had just been imagining this shit all these years.

"You know what the fuck I'm talking about!" I shouted, keeping my hand firmly on the gun. "Ever since I met yo' ass, little miss Aaliyah could do no wrong. Do you know what it's been like living in yo' fucking shadow all these years? I go around my own damn family and they ask about you."

"Where is all of this coming from?"

"You've always had, Aaliyah. You were the apple of your dad's eye while I merely just existed for mine. Yes my dad loved me, but he showed me with money, not by physically being there. Then as soon as the man of my dreams comes along, pays me a little attention, you swoop in and take him from me too."

"Girl, if you ain't have this gun on me I swear I'd sit down and try to wrap my head around this shit you saying. I came in and took Meko from you? Yea, I must've hit yo' ass hard as hell years ago because you losing your fucking mind."

"Yea, you can play dumb all you want, but you and I both know what Meko and I shared, and now you can look at my son every day and know that we shared him as well. So just remember if you kill me, I'll still live on through that kid outside."

"You remember what our fathers always taught us right? If you're gonna pull your gun…"

"Be prepare to shoot," I finished her sentence just as we both pulled the trigger, only mine hit the window while hers connected, hitting my chest. I heard the door open and close again. Unlike the first time, I knew there would be no reincarnation. I was headed to meet my maker. I just wish I could've made amends with my mom and son before I closed my eyes.

Elijah

Hearing a shot come from the house I jumped and so did the Uber driver. I put my head down knowing what had just happened.

"Young man, what is going on?" he asked in his thick Indian accent.

"Everything's cool man, my aunt is coming out in a minute," I said the first thing that came to my mind. The driver looked skeptical, but he made sure to stay put. Before he could say anything else, Aaliyah came walking out of the house. By the look on her face I could tell that the shot we heard was the official demise of my mother.

"We're going back to the airstrip where you picked us up," Aaliyah told the driver who pulled off in that direction. She gave me a look that told me what I needed to know without me even asking. I let my tears fall freely down my face. I was no longer the tough fourteen-year-old I portrayed in the beginning. I was a lost child. I cried tears for my grandmother and tears for me. Unsure of what was going on with Shawn, I had no one to go home to. As we boarded the plane I took a seat near the window.

"When I was younger my grandmother used to show me home videos of my mom and tell me stories about her. She told me she did that so that I could keep those memories and know how full of life she was. Most kids grow up without one parent in the home, for me it was both. That was rough in itself, but to now know that my mom was alive all this time and didn't think to just pop in on me every once in a while to show me that she at least cared, hurts the most. I can tell by the way you looked at me when you first got in the car that my mom is dead, you don't have to tell me. Now I have no one." I turned to look at Aaliyah and she too had tears coming down her face.

"Your mom and I were like frick and frack when we were younger. I could have never foreseen our lives taking this kind of turn. I'm not some heartless killer. If I was you'd have been dead a long time ago. Believe it or not, as sure as Eli King Sr.'s blood runs through you, you are my family." I wanted to accept the open invitation to being a part of the Jones clan, but how could I consciously sleep at night knowing that it was her fault that I was an orphan in the first place? Deciding to leave the conversation where it was, I leaned against the window and slept until we arrived back in NY.

Getting off the plane, I saw Shawn's car parked at the strip with him standing in front of it. Aaliyah gave me a slight smile before getting off the plane. I assumed this was her way of extending an olive branch. Nothing could replace my gma but at least I wouldn't be alone; I guess.

"Wassup man," Shawn greeted me with a manly hug.

"Hey, I'm going with you?"

"Yea, go get in the car while I talk to Aaliyah real quick." Looking back at Aaliyah for the final time, I walked away and got in his car. I watched as they talked for a few minutes before she threw her hands up and hopped in her car speeding off.

"Yo, I know shit is all bad right now, but you can stay with me and I'ma hold you down. I can't say that I know what you going through because I don't, just know I got you man. You wanna go to ya house and get some stuff?"

"Nah, I can't go back there." I couldn't bear going back home knowing my gma wasn't there. I wasn't ready to face Tim and tell him what happened. It was all good just a week ago. Shit was all bad now, I gotta fix it.

"Aight, we going to my crib. It's just me and you now kid."

A year had passed since my gma was killed and I was a shell of the person I once was. I became consumed with anger and hatred for Aaliyah. Even more so now than when I wanted revenge for my mom. Life seemed harder now, granted Shawn did what he could to make me comfortable. I was taken care of as far as shelter, food, and clothing, but he didn't have the ability to help me with coping skills. I had even gone so far as to drop out of school. I started hanging in the same hood that Will would slang out of and became the kid that just didn't give a fuck.

"Yo, we gotta do something about the path you're going down Eli. You out here fucking up, we gon' have CPS on our asses. You got me thinking we went through all this shit with the courts for nothing bro," Shawn was on my ass soon as I came in the house as usual.

"Man, ain't nobody tryna hear that shit. You plugged, make the courts believe that I'm being home schooled or some shit," I retorted. I was tired of hearing him talk shit about how I was living my life. He constantly stressed about me getting back in school and about the crew I was hanging with. He wasn't my damn daddy. Heading into the kitchen, I opened the fridge to grab something to eat. I didn't hear him walk up on me until he pushed the fridge closed and pushed me against it.

"Listen lil' nigga, I know I've been leaving you to your own vices because I thought that you could manage without me breathing down your back. Now I know you're still grieving your grandmother and ya mama, but you got me fucked up if you think I'ma keep turning a blind eye to ya bullshit. You keep forgetting that I have the power to turn the lights out on that lil' block that you hanging out on. Don't take me letting you go through this phase as me being a punk ass nigga, 'cause I'm not." I went to move but he pushed me back again. "Now, yo' little ass is going back to school even if I have to sit in the classes with you myself, ya feel me? You think yo' grandmother would want you out here on the block wasting yo' life?"

The mention of my gma pissed me off. "You think she would be okay with you still fucking with Aaliyah? Man, don't act like you give a fuck about me. You prolly only doing all this for me just to make yourself feel good. I don't need ya help, I don't need nobody!" I hauled off and punched the wall leaving a whole. I wanted to cry, but no tears came out. Shit was fucked up; I was fucked up and I didn't know how to express it. We faced off in the kitchen, me breathing hard and squeezing my fist and him just staring at me.

"You need to speak with someone about how you feeling. You have a lot of built up anger and while granted, you not channeling that shit into nothing positive. You see how you just wild out, that shit ain't cool and it's not safe."

"Whatever you say man. You want me to go back to school I'll go, but I don't need to talk to nobody about nothing. I've been dealing with these feelings by myself this long." Grabbing a bottle of water I walked back out the same way I came in. I wasn't feeling Shawn trying to play Dr. Phil. I appreciated how he was trying to look out for me, but nobody could tell me how to mourn. I needed to play the block to clear my head. Requesting an Uber from the app on my phone, I waited the five minutes in the lobby for it to arrive. When it pulled up I got in.

"Elijah?" the woman verified.

"Yes," I confirmed my identity and we drove off. During the ride I plugged in my ear pods and I zoned out to "I'll be Missing You" by Diddy and the Family. Whenever I was having a rough day such as this one, I went right to this song and it put me in a place where I thought about the good times with my gma. No matter how much time had gone by, I still missed her terribly. Feeling the car stop we were now at my destination, building three ten. I had hung out with Will around here on multiple occasions and every so often I'd see my mom's cousins and we'd share a hi and bye. Thanking the driver, I got out and dapped up the crowd of guys that stood in front of the building.

"Eli," I heard my name being called. Looking past the crowd I saw TT waving me over. She was one of my mom's cousins that I'd see when I was on the block.

"Wassup TT," I said once I made it through the crowd.

"Hey boo, how you holding up?"

"I'm hanging in there under the circumstances." I hated when people asked me that. How the hell did they think I was doing? My life had been turned upside down and I was still trying to find my way.

"So look, we both have a mutual hate for a certain Aaliyah King and I've found a way to rid us of our problem."

"I'm good on that." I had lost so much going after Aaliyah and her family I had learned my lesson. I was content with hating her from afar. Plus, I didn't want my sister to have to feel this pain that I lived through every day if her mother was killed. TT looked shocked and disappointed with my response.

"Damn, you and Shawn drinking that same potion. I guess she has to actually shoot yo' ass for you to see how cutthroat she is. You walking around here basically an orphan now that your grandmother is dead and you don't want blood?"

"Nah, I wanna live to be able to experience the memories of my gma, not die in vain. Plus I have Shawn to hold me down too." She shook her head before walking off. Looking up in the sky I spoke to my gma, something I did often when I felt her spirit.

Gma, I'm not sure where I'm headed or what all this means. I know when you pulled me out of the mission you did it for a reason. I just wish we had more time; I needed more time. Shawn has been doing the best he can so I'ma start meeting him halfway and be the greatness I was destined to be. I love and I miss you lady. I'ma get it right, I promise.

Shawn

I didn't expect to become a parent overnight once Eli stepped off that plane with Liyah a year ago. I didn't know about his grandmother until he told me and I was shocked to hear that Erica had been alive the whole time. He was fucked up behind the death of his grandmother and I tried to be there as much as I could, but clearly I was failing. He had become a handful and between running the streets trying to go legit and looking after him, I didn't know whether I was coming or going. I started the process to cleaning up my money and getting out the game so that I could set a better example. That lil' nigga was making it hard to be understanding.

Today I was fed up. I had received yet another call from his school's guidance counselor letting me know he had been out of school for a while. I wouldn't have known seeing as his slick ass would always leave the house early in the morning and come back after school hours. The guidance counselor had been working with him to help get him back on track, but his words of encouragement did nothing. When he broke down a little while ago I was hoping this was his breakthrough.

While I had to figure out my home situation with Eli I also was working out salvaging what was left of a relationship with Liyah. We had been talking, but she had put a pause on the whole rekindling our unspoken relationship. I picked up my phone to call her and see what she was up to. The phone rang a couple times before I hung up. This was normal, I'd call and sometimes she'd answer, other times she wouldn't. I couldn't trip though. After what happened with Emery she had been very closed off. My phone then rang and it was her calling back.

"Wassup ma," I answered on the third ring. I couldn't have her thinking I was waiting by the phone for her to return the call.

"Hey love," she spoke in an upbeat voice. "Sorry I missed your call."

"It's cool, I was just checking in with you."

"Bad day?" She caught on to my flat tone.

"Something like that."

"Care to share?"

"That's what I need to be asking you. Can you share some of your parenting tips? I swear I'm doing a piss poor job over here with Eli man." She became quiet. I didn't take into consideration that this might not be a subject she wanted to touch on. "My bad, that may not be a conversation we should be having, huh?"

"I'm okay with it if you are. I was going to ask you how he was doing anyway." Since she asked I went on to tell her about what we were dealing with and how I was at a crossroads about my decision to become his sole guardian. "Well, I can't tell you that I'm an expert at this parenting thing. You know I'm still getting the hang of it myself. What I will say is the last thing you wanna do is give up on him. He's gone through a traumatic experience at such a young age and right now he doesn't know which way to go. I gotta say it was an honorable decision for you to make to take him in. Let him know that you're there for him and you got his back no matter what. That's what he needs right now, that confirmation."

Everything she said made sense. I had been basically leaving him to his own vices, thinking nothing was wrong because he never said anything. Eli was young, but very smart. He was able to mask the hurt that he felt very well up until today. I needed to sit down and listen to him. Of course he needed to get back in school and stay off the block, but I wanted him to know that I was here.

"Thanks for that. You've helped more than you know. I wanna pull up on you in a few. I haven't seen that beautiful face of yours in a while." The last time I'd seen her was about two months ago and that was for a quickie. For every itch she needed scratched, I was right there.

"That would be nice." I could hear the smile in her voice. "I'm going to send you my address." She was inviting me to the crib, now this was a step in the right direction. After making plans to see each other in a few, I got ready to hit the block to find Eli. Before I could make it out the door, he was coming in.

"Just the man I wanted to see."

"Before you say anything, I wanna apologize." He shocked me, but I let him continue. "I was wrong for flipping out, but this shit ain't easy for me. I know I gotta get on the right track and I plan to."

"Look, I know I ain't ya moms or ya pops and I know I can't replace your grandmother. I'm just ya cousin and I'm still tryna take this parenting shit day by day. All I ask is that you work with me and stop doing this dumb shit you doing 'cause you better than that. I know it and you know it. If you going through something come politic with a nigga so we can figure that shit out together. I'ma tell you what nobody ever told me, the block ain't yo' friend. Get back into yo' studies so you can make ya grandma proud and shit, you feel me?" He nodded his head in understanding and I dapped him up.

"I'ma 'bout to head out for a few. Order some food and I'll see you a little later, aight?" Dapping him again I started out to Liyah's house. On the way I stopped by the mall to pick her up some roses and a bracelet from Cartier as a thinking of you gift. Since Pam was killed I had been bringing in ten times more money than I had before. Why not spend it on my lady? Yea, I still claimed her because like I said before, this was only a pause.

After Pam was killed I found out from one of the block boys that Will was the one that shot me a little while ago. Even though my grandma had told me that he was up to some bullshit with Pam, I never thought my man's since elementary school would try to take me out. Then again, look how my cousin had done her best friend. Liyah confirmed what I had heard in the streets when she said she ran in the house to get Emi and Will was there. My boy went out bad man. The world was wicked, it be the ones you closest to ready and willing to take you out.

Liyah had done well for herself. Pulling up to her mini mansion I was impressed. I remembered when she showed me the layout of the place a while back during the building stage. Parking my car I got out and jogged up the three steps to the door. Ringing the doorbell, I was taken aback by her attire.

"Hey, come on in," she said out of breath.

"The hell you got going on in here ma? You all sweaty and shit." She still looked good as fuck though. She chuckled, closing the door behind me.

"I was working out. Come on, I'm doing Zumba in the living room." She pulled me by my arm and I followed.

"Them ain't no workout clothes, those is twerk out clothes." I grabbed at the little ass spandex shorts she had on and sports bra that smuggled her melon-sized breasts. I could clearly see her pussy print through the shorts, but I wasn't complaining.

"You silly, you tryna get down on this Zumba with me?" she asked with her hand on her hips like she was challenging me. I looked up at the flat screen tv that hung over a fireplace and noticed how much the people were sweating on the video and instantly decided I was good.

"Nope. You so into yo' twerk out you didn't notice I came bearing gifts." I lifted up the bag for her to see.

"Oh shit, I'm sorry. Aww what's this?" She grabbed the bag, smiling big. I watched as she opened it in excitement. Taking out the bracelet, she examined it closely. "Bling bling, every time I come around yo' city, bling bling." Putting the bracelet on her wrist, she waved it in the air quoting lyrics from the Cash Money group The Hot Boys. I laughed at her extra ass.

"I did good, huh?"

"You did great love." And there I was back in the game. Leaning over, she kissed my lips softly, making my nature rise. Reaching over me she used the remote to mute the workout video. "Alexa, play *'Dance for You'* by Beyoncé." *I just wanna, show you how much I appreciate you, yes. Wanna show you how much I'm dedicated to you, yes. Wanna show you how much I will foreva be true. Wanna show you how much you got yo' girl feelin' good, oh yes.* She danced slowly to the music, sensually, while removing her workout gear.

"Come put that pussy on my face." I didn't care about the sweat; I was being a nasty nigga tonight. I lifted her up and her pussy rested right where I needed to be. I feasted on her until she screamed my name and begged me to put her down. I did as she asked only I sat her on the couch and relatched onto her, not being able to get enough of her.

"Ooh, ooh, shit yess." She thrusted her hips on my tongue as she came again. Knowing I didn't want her to give out on me, I stood up. Not giving me a chance to do anything else, she grabbed my face and kissed me nastily and with urgency. As much as I wanted to give her this dick 'til her clit was hanging out of her pussy lips, I stopped.

"Hol' up ma, hol' up." I lifted off of her and sat back on the couch with my eyes closed.

"What? What's wrong?" My dick was on hard, but my mind wanted to know what the fuck was happening here. Opening my eyes, I looked over at her and she was sitting up on her elbows looking dead at me.

"I could knock ya socks off right now, but I really need to know what's going on with us." Normally I wasn't the guy that was in touch with his emotions, but with Aliyah shit was different. Instead of responding she started to re-dress. I took that as an indication that the conversation I was tryna have with her was off the table, so I got up to leave. "I'ma see you, aight?"

"Well damn, did you want me to answer the question?" she asked as she sat back down on the couch.

"Oh, yeah, I thought, never mind go 'head." I sat next to her awaiting her response.

"You already know this past year since I've been released has been eventful. I didn't expect to come home and be received by everyone with open arms. I also didn't expect to be so hated that I would be shot at on the day of my release and my daughter would be kidnapped in the time span of a couple months. I appreciate you still rocking with me after all that. Of course I wanna be with you; shit, who wouldn't after all that? I just don't wanna have to look over my shoulder when it comes to ya family. How do I know that no one else is gonna want revenge? You already know once anyone comes for me and my family it's either me or them, and I can almost promise it won't be me."

Like Eli, this was the first time she had given me the real on how she felt. I wasn't surprised at how she felt; at least now we could discuss it. I pulled her onto my lap, where she was facing me with her legs wrapped around my waist. I needed her to understand and hear what I was about to tell her.

"I hear you and I wish you would've said something sooner. I can assure you that you don't have to worry about that shit if you give me a fair chance. While I can't control my family and their feelings, I can control what I allow in my space. People know how I'm coming behind you. Hell, I've been that way from the day I saw you." She chuckled, knowing I was telling nothing but the truth. "I want this." I motioned between the two of us. "I ain't saying it's gonna be easy, but

I can tell you it's gonna be worth it." I meant everything I said and was willing to show her.

"Okay, let's see where this goes," she said, skeptical. I was fine with her skepticism though. I was going hard for mine.

Emery

"Emery, I wanna let you go, but you know I can't."

"I don't know shit, but that you're a fucking coward Dre. This shit is wrong and you know it."

"You think I wanna do this shit to you? Man, I was forced into this shit." I wasn't trying to hear anything Dre had to say. I had been beaten and threatened, quite frankly I was over it.

"Emi Ice, you okay babygirl? You've been sitting at this table since you got here." I lifted my head to find Ms. Emma standing in front of me. I had been sitting in a daze in the kitchen at my pop's house.

"Umm, yea I'm okay, just zoned out for a moment. Is Pop upstairs?" She nodded her head yes and I got up to go see him.

I noticed I'd been doing that a lot lately. Even though it had been the better part of a year, those couple days of being held captive still shook me to this day. The goal was to act and think tough so that Dre didn't think the whole ordeal was getting to me, when in fact it was. I put on a front for my family like everything was good, but in all honesty I had been carrying these thoughts with me trying to sort them out as best as I could.

"Hey Pop, what you doing?" I jumped on my grandfather's bed where he sat up reading the paper.

"Reading up on current events babygirl. What you up to? It's nice out. I figured you'd be running the streets with Porscha."

"Nah, not today. I came over to ask your opinion on something. I'm a little conflicted."

"Talk to me." He sat the paper next to him and gave me his undivided attention.

"I've been thinking about reaching out to Eli to see how he's doing." I waited for him to object, when he didn't, I continued. "I just feel different after what I went through, you know. I can't imagine how he feels losing his security blanket. The least I can do as a big sister is be there for him." I had been feeling this way for a while now and trying to find the best way to address it. I hadn't seen or heard from Eli since the day I was rescued.

Looking in his eyes that day I could tell he was hurt for me. It seemed like whatever plan was set wasn't supposed to include me in that magnitude. I came to my pop because I knew he'd give me sound advice with no emotion.

"What does your heart say?"

"It says I am my brother's keeper," I responded with confidence. He nodded his head and went back to reading his paper. That was his way of saying he was okay with my decision. Now I had to execute. The next day I decided to pop up on Eli at his house. I got the address from my mom, who was hopeful and happy about me reaching out to him. She let me know that despite how he may have felt about her, she didn't want to hinder our relationship. Arriving at the building he lived in, I noticed a boy who looked like Eli walking in.

"Eli," I called out his name, hoping I was right and didn't just embarrass myself. The kid turned around and it was him. I rolled my window down further and leaned out of it. "Wassup bro." Surprisingly, he smiled at me before walking over to the car.

"What's good Emi, how's everything?"

"Everything is everything. I came to check up on you. You mind if I come up so we can have a big sis/lil' bro chat?" I asked, hopeful that he was willing to hear what I had to say.

"Sure, you can't park here though. Come around and park in the garage." I followed his instructions to park and went into the building. We rode the elevator in silence, me thinking about what I wanted to say to him. Walking into the penthouse apartment, I looked around taking in how clean it was for two guys to be living here.

"So wassup, what you wanna talk about?" he asked, taking a seat on the couch, and pointed to the love seat across from it for me to sit.

"Well damn, can I get something to drink or something? I gotta teach you some manners," I joked, and he laughed. I wanted to lighten the mood.

"Girl, the fridge is stocked with all kinds of shit, help yourself." I went to the fridge and he was right, it was stocked. Organized too. As a matter of fact, it looked just like my fridge at home. I automatically knew my mom had something to do with it.

"You know my mother organized this fridge, right?" I grabbed a water and sat back down.

"Oh yeah? I figured it wasn't Shawn, it was too organized." I snickered and took a sip of my water.

"I came over here today because ever since everything went down I've been thinking about you. Not on no weird shit though. I know when we initially crossed paths you were getting close to me on some get-back shit. I was thinking that we could start fresh, this time with good intentions." He sat up straight from his laid back positioned on the couch and stared as if he was trying to figure me out. "I mean, when you really think about it, neither one of us were in the position to give the other a fair chance."

"Yea, you're right. I think it would be cool and it'll make our dad proud." The mention of our father didn't move me. Not that I didn't have love for him, because according to my mother he loved me to death, I just didn't think about him. "I never got to say this, but I'm sorry for what happened to you. Like you said in the beginning, I tried to get close to you to get to ya mom. I swear I had nothing to do with the plan to kidnap you; that shit was foul." While I appreciated the apology I didn't want to relive that day with him. I did that enough on my own.

"Thank you. And I'm sorry about what this madness did to you." I had to choose my words wisely. I wasn't sorry for what was done to his grandma nor his fake dead ass mammy. As far as I was concerned, they got what they deserved. I couldn't say that to him though. "I know it's gonna take a minute before you can forgive my mom. Just know she's a good person who was put in a fucked up position." He nodded his head, not putting words to his thoughts. I was okay with that. Things were still pretty fresh so some wounds were hard to close.

I planned to go into this brother and sistership with an open mind. I wanted to know that I could trust him and vice versa. It was important for us to establish some kind of understanding. At the end of the day, we were bonded by blood.

"Aight, the first thing we gonna do to kick off this bro and sis thing is shopping," I said excitedly.

"Uh uh, no we ain't. We 'bout to watch this game. Golden State is playing the Raptors and I wanna see that nigga Drake act a fool over his team."

"Well why you ain't say Drake was involved, that's daddy. Go 'head and put it on," I encouraged while moving next to him on the couch. Drake was my man, so if he had anything to do with this game I was here for it.

"You know what, on second thought, I did see some new Jay's I wanted to pick up at the mall. Let's go blow a bag." He turned the tv off and got up to walk to the door.

"Yo' hating ass." I giggled while walking out of the door he held open for me. I decided on Westchester Mall since they had a bigger selection than the local stores. On the drive there I noticed we had the same taste in music. We bobbed our heads to PNB Rock's *"Put You On"* featuring A Boogie. He rapped the lyrics word for word like he wrote the song. We arrived at the mall and I texted my mom to let her know where I was. She didn't even respond back; instead, she FaceTimed me.

Parking the car I answered, "Yea Ma?"

She moved her head around in the camera looking for Eli. I turned the phone towards him and he gave her a head nod. I watched as she waved back and smiled at the first step for Eli toward burying his ill feelings. Turning the camera back to me my mom smiled big and gave a thumbs up before disconnecting the call. "Okay lil' bro, let's do this."

In the mall I looked on as he picked up multiple items, even more than me. For someone who was anti mall a minute ago, he sure was swiping away. After much shopping we both worked up an appetite. Stopping at the food court for a bite to eat, he grabbed a table that was big enough for us and our bags. While eating a woman approached the table and spoke to Eli.

"Hey Eli, what you doing out here?" the woman asked.

"I'm here with my sister," he nodded towards me, making the woman frown. Now I respected my elders, but I'd be damned if I was disrespected.

"Hmph, ya sister, huh?"

"Yes, his sister," I confirmed with much attitude. She went to say something else, but Eli interrupted before she could.

"This is my dad's daughter." Looking back at me, she nodded her head and walked off.

"What the hell was that about and who was that?" I asked, now ready to leave the mall. Something about ol' girl didn't sit right with me.

"That's my cousin TT. She's been on bullshit ever since my mom got killed." He brushed it off. I, on the other hand, was on high alert. I paid more attention as we left the mall and loaded our bags into my car. I made sure to store her name in my mental rolodex to mention to my mom later. I dropped Eli off home with promises to link again soon. Overall, I had a good time with him and I was confident that we'd hang out more often. As often as siblings usually hung out.

Getting on the highway to head back home, I felt like someone was following me. As I weaved in and out of traffic, the person followed one car behind, confirming my suspicions. Grabbing my phone, I dialed my mom on speaker. Staying calm, I paid attention to the road and explained what was going on.

"Ma, don't panic, I believe I'm being followed. No, I know for a fact I'm being followed," I corrected myself as the car switched into another lane with me.

"Where are you right now Emi?"

"I'm on the Westside Highway, headed home. I just dropped Eli off."

"Okay, I want you to get off and head Uptown to the shop. I'm here waiting on you. When you get here don't get out of the car. I'm going to come out to you." I nodded my head silently in understanding of her instructions. "Emi Ice," she bellowed. "Did you hear what I said?"

"Yes Ma, I'm about ten minutes out from the shop. The person is still one car behind me."

"Okay, stay on the phone with me and keep your eyes on the road." Keeping my eyes focused on the road, I stole glances in the rearview mirror as the car tried to blend in with others. That was the first major fail seeing as though the car was burnt orange. The driver had to have been following me since I pulled off from dropping Eli. *What the fuck is going on?* I thought to myself.

"Ma, I'm outside," I announced, parking in front of the shop. My mother came out just as the car sped off. Now seeing it in full view, I noticed the side profile of a woman driving the Chrysler 300. Using my phone I quickly snapped a picture of it, but unfortunately the driver sped off so quick I missed the license plate.

"Was that the car?" my mother asked while leaning in my window. I nodded my head yes. "Who all did you see at the mall today?"

"Nobody important, oh except for Eli's cousin TT." She opened my car door and motioned for me to get out. We both headed into the shop, not before I noticed how her eyes had glazed over. For the next hour I watched as my mom went about the day like nothing had happened, but I knew better. There was a reason that car followed me. As we locked up the shop for the night, I helped her count the register.

"Emi, did TT say anything to you earlier?"

"Not really, she spoke to Eli. She tried to shade me when he mentioned that I was his sister; that was about it."

"Okay," she responded flatly.

"Ma, what's going on?"

"I'm not sure, but trust and believe I'm gonna find out." *Shit, what now?*

Aaliyah

All I wanted to do was come home and live my best life, but it seemed as if that was never going to happen. At this point I felt like I was gonna have to wipe out Erica's entire bloodline just to protect my own. I had no concrete proof that it was TT that followed Emi a couple days ago, but it sure was no coincidence that she popped up at the mall. This was exactly why I told Shawn that a relationship with him and I would not work. Granted I had grown to love him but shit, how was he going to keep loving me if I kept taking out his family members?

"What you over here thinking about ma?" Shawn asked as we laid out on the couch watching tv.

"Nothing, I thought you were sleeping." I had yet to tell him anything about the incident with Emi because I wanted to see how things were gonna play out.

"I was, your thoughts woke me up." I looked at him confused before smiling. "Yea ma, I'm in tune with you, so tell me what's going on." I got up and walked through the living room into the kitchen.

"You want something to eat?" I was trying my best to avoid having to bring the incident up.

"Nah, I'm full from earlier," he winked. "Stop trying to avoid my question though." I sighed before telling him about Emi being followed. I left out the part about me thinking it was TT that followed her. Some things you have to leave to yourself, and this was one of them.

"Why you just now telling me that? Is she good, did she see the person?" I assured him that Emi was fine and that she didn't see anyone. He had gotten closer to her this past year and they had formed their own bond outside of me. "Look, is there any way she can be driven from now on when she goes out? Something not sitting well with me and it's not my place to tell her what she can and can't do." I could appreciate his concern for her. It let me know that he was growing to love my child and that was a plus for me.

"I'm already a step ahead of you. I have a driver that's been checked out who's going to get her where she needs to go and ensure her safe trip back home."

"Aight cool, come here a minute," he motioned with his finger for me to come to him. I did and sat on his lap. "You know you gotta give me a baby soon, right?" I laughed him off, but he didn't crack a smile.

"You serious, huh?"

"Yea, Emi is practically grown. We need a little one running around here." I just shook my head. With the way things were going with him and I, that was very possible. Only I had to ensure that all of my enemies were taken care of. TT had added herself to that list.

"Come on, let's go out to eat instead." I changed the subject, getting up to get dressed. Of course I wanted to eat Ruth's Chris so that's where we decided to go. Looking over at Shawn as he drove, I felt nothing but love. He had come into my life and embraced me with open arms through everything. Even throughout this year after Emi's kidnapping I tried to keep him at bay, but he held it down. I hadn't felt this kind of love since the happy times with Eli.

It's crazy because I could have never seen this coming. I spent fourteen years in jail for killing my husband and my best friend. Speaking of Erica, my mind was still blown at the fact that she had been alive all these years. The day Elijah and I had shown up on her doorstep she looked great, as if she didn't have a care in the world. It was also right there where I realized that her love for Eli had outweighed her parental instinct. That whole time she tried to persuade me that I had taken something from her that was never hers to begin with. It amazed me how she really believed that.

Arriving at Ruth's Chris, Shawn got out first before opening up my door and helping me out. I placed a juicy kiss on his lips and closed the passenger side door. He looked at me strange, and I laughed.

"What was that for?"

"Just because I love you boo."

"Oh yeah?"

"Yep, come on, I'm hungry." I pulled at his arm.

"Wait, hold up. Do you love me enough to come with me to my grandma's birthday party she's throwing herself?"

"Nope," I said without any thought before walking into the restaurant. That was an absolute no for me. The waitress walked me to my table where Shawn came in soon after. I buried my face in the menu, not wanting to look at him. I hated to be so short, I just didn't see me being around his family any time soon.

"So you just gon' leave a nigga outside like fuck me huh. What if somebody would've taken me?" he joked and I snickered. Leave it to him to make me laugh when I was in my feelings.

"Whatever, what you ordering?"

"You order for us and then we gon' talk about what I asked you." The waitress came over and I ordered the same meal I had on our "first date." I wasn't interested in having this conversation, but I would oblige him. Our food came quickly and I tore into mine. He took little bites and waited for me to finish. "So can we talk now that you've stuffed ya face?"

"You and I both know that's not a good idea Shawn, so what do we really need to talk about?"

"Grandma don't have an issue with you though."

"Unless ya grandmother is throwing a party for three which includes you and I, I'm not interested." I would be a fool to go over there amongst all those people looking at me sideways. Then I'd have to be looking over my shoulder and shit. Nope, I was good.

And here I was, the fucking fool on my way to the party in the back park at three ten. I took Emi with me to meet up with Shawn and Eli who were already there. Eli and Emi had been hanging out more often and I was happy about it. He still hadn't come around to the idea of being in my presence for long, but he did speak when he was. I learned to take what I could get. Parking in the back park I sat in my car for a moment to get ready for what was to come.

"Ma, you sure about this?" Emi asked while checking her face in the visor. We were having a mommy and me moment in our sun dresses only different colors.

"Honestly, no I'm not, but I'm gonna make the best of it for the sake of Shawn."

"I give it to you ma, you're a better woman than me. I'd be like I'm good, holla at me when you leaving up outta there." I laughed at her chucking up the deuces. "You really love Shawn huh?"

"I do, so come on and let's show up for my future husband." She smiled and I took that as her approval. Getting out of the car, we followed the music that played loudly in the background. When we got in the park the party was in full swing. Everyone from the block had come out to celebrate Grandma Janet's seventy-first birthday. Emi stayed closed to me, not in a weird way, but more cautious than anything. Approaching the crowd, Grandma Janet was in the middle dancing to 50 Cent's *"In Da Club."*

Go go go go, go shawty it's ya birthday, we gon' party like it's ya birthday, we gon' sip Bacardi like it's ya birthday. And you know we don't give a fuck it's not ya birthday. The DJ mixed the chorus about four times before he let the full song play. The crowd went crazy once Grandma dropped it to the floor before bringing it back up with no help. I looked over to Emi who was in awe herself. That was Janet for you, as youthful as ever. I saw Shawn through the crowd and we locked eyes as he walked over to us. Hugging Emi, he kissed my lips twice and smiled.

"You the shit for this, you know that right?"

"Yea I know. You can show me just how thankful you are for my presence when we get back to the house tonight." I winked and he licked his lips, making me tingle.

"Umm, y'all do know I'm still standing right here, right? Like right here in front of y'all," Emi pointed out with her face twisted up. We chuckled and pulled away from each other a little. Shawn waived Eli over who was talking amongst a crowd of young boys. He gave me a hello and hugged Emi. As the crowd dispersed Janet approached us.

"Well hey pretty girl, I gotta hunt you down for you to come see me," she said with a hand on her hip. "Come over here and give me a hug chile, stop playing." I walked into her open arms and she hugged me just as she had done so many times before. "I've always believed you Liyah. Let that burden you're carrying go," she whispered in my ear making me tear up. She held me while I wiped my eyes.

Pulling back from her, I mouthed the words *thank you*, and she nodded her head. She also embraced Emi. During the whole party I got a couple stares, but people I'd known when I visited the building gave me hugs and welcomed me home. I was enjoying myself and so did Emi who was dancing with the neighborhood kids. As the night started to slow down the music shifted to a lot of old school cuts. I let Shawn know I was ready to take it in.

"Aight ma, let me go say goodnight to Grandma and let Eli know we out." Locking arms with Emi I got ready to head to my car.

"Look at this bitch here. She kills my cousin and then shows up to our family function," a drunk TT slurred. Handing Emi my keys, I told her to go to the car. She didn't answer quickly, just stood there next to me. Giving her a nudge, I shoved the keys in her hand and pointed to the car. The look I gave let her know this wasn't up for debate.

"You drunk and this is your grandmother's birthday party, so I'ma let you have that." Here I was trying to avoid yet another confrontation that found me.

"TT, let's go." Her sister pulled at her arm and she yanked away.

"No, that's the problem right there. Y'all let her get away with killing Erica and now y'all want me to be quiet about it."

"Is that why you following my daughter around? 'Cause you tryna get some kind of payback?" I wanted to bait her into admitting that she was the one who Emi saw following her days ago.

"Fuck you and your daughter. Let me go Qiana!" As she raised her voice a crowd formed around us. And this was what I didn't want. I watched as Shawn walked over with Eli following close behind him. He went over to TT in an attempt to get her to calm down and walk it off. Eli came over and stood next to me. I guess he was picking sides again, which threw TT in an uproar. "You little fucking bastard, she killed your mother, what are you doing?" she shouted at him.

"Tiana bring yo' ass over here and stop all that nonsense," Janet barked, making her calm down a little and walk off, but not before slapping Shawn's hand off of her. He just stood there shaking his head. I decided to walk off as well. TT and I would have our moment and it wouldn't be pretty. Before I could take a step I heard a pop and a burning sensation in my back.

"Maaaaaa," a blood curdling scream came from Emi before I hit the ground and everything went black around me.

"You can't be here." I turned to see who was talking and Meko was standing to the side of me in all white.

"Meko?" I looked at him then down at myself and it looked as if I was floating.

"Yea shawty, it's me. Look, you can't be here." For the first time in fifteen years, I cried for him. He looked the same, and you couldn't even see the bullet hole from where I had shot him.

"Why you do me like that Meko? I loved you, you were my air. We were supposed to grow old together, raise Emery. How you fuck it up like that?" I didn't try to mask my hurt. I let the tears fall and bared my soul. He moved closer to me and grasped my hands in his. His hands were soft, almost like a baby's. A stark contrast from the rough hands he had while we were together.

"It was never my intention to hurt you the way I did. You were and still are the best thing that ever happened to me. I couldn't tell you why what happened between Erica and I happened, I was caught up." His eyes got cloudy and I knew he had started to cry as well, but he caught the tear just before it could fall down his cheeks. "You gotta go back and be there for our daughter and please lookout for my son. Oh, and get that bitch TT." Before I could say anything else he disappeared.

"Somebody better tell me something right fucking now!" I heard my father bark.

"Oh god, Liyah baby we're here." I identified the voice as Ms. Emma's. Tears fell on my face and I wanted to reach up and wipe them, but I couldn't. What the fuck was going on? Where was Emi? As if she could hear my thoughts, I heard Emi's voice telling me she was here and squeezing my arm.

"Doc, what the fuck is the prognosis? You not talking right now is not a good look for you, and it determines whether or not you're gonna live for the next twenty-four hours." My dad's voice went up another octave and I wanted so bad to be able to talk, so that I could tell the doctor to say something.

"Babe, come on, let me talk to the doctor. You go over there to Shawn

and find out what happened. Please babe, do that for me, I got this." Yes Lou, take over before he gets y'all kicked out, I thought to myself. *While Lou talked to the doctor Ms. Emma prayed over me. I could hear Emi's soft cries and that was enough for me to get my ass up.*

"I'm right here Emi Ice," I whispered and squeezed her hand.

"Ma," she called out in a child-like voice before wrapping her arms around my neck and squeezing me tightly. I blocked out the sharp pain that went through my body and allowed her to hug me. I looked around to see where Shawn was, but he wasn't in the room. Reaching out for Ms. Emma who had fresh tears streaming from her eyes, I asked for Shawn.

"He's out there talking to your dad boo," Lou answered for her. "Let me go get them. I'm so happy you're alive." She rushed out of the room and returned seconds later with the guys. The look on my dad's face said it all. He was not happy and seeing me in this condition was set to bring out the worst in him. Shawn had a solemn look on his face. I know he must've felt like he failed me, but he had no way of knowing this would happen.

"Babygirl, you scared your old man. It was touch and go for a second. How are you feeling?" My dad came over and replaced Emi at the side of my bed, kissing my forehead.

"I've seen better days. You know they can't keep a real one down though. Babe, why you standing way over there like I'm made of porcelain? Come over here, I promise I won't break." I used the remote beside my bed and pressed a button for me to sit up. The pain that shot through my back had me immediately regretting my decision. "Ooh fuck," I groaned out in pain.

"Chill ma, I'm right here." Shawn's voice did nothing to ease my pain. My back was on fire and it was at that moment I remembered that I had been shot in the back. He leaned into me, whispering in my ear. "I can't tell you how sorry I am and I'm willing to spend a lifetime making this shit up to you." I grabbed his face in my hands and placed a kiss on his lips. It was my way of telling him I didn't blame him for what happened.

"Okay, now that we got that out of the way, I still need to know who did this and I'll take care of the rest," my dad spoke with authority, and I knew his words were final. "I'm tired of this shit and I've sat back long enough. It's time that I stepped in and made the streets feel me." TT would be taken care of just like the others had, and I'd be the one to do it, not him.

My fifth day in the hospital, I asked that everyone go home so I could have a few moments to myself. At least that's what I wanted them to think. I actually planned on checking myself out today. The doctor tried to fight me on it, telling me I needed more rest; I wasn't trying to hear it. After finding out the bullet that hit me missed my spine by a few inches, I knew it was God on my side. Lifting up from my position from the bed I pulled myself up to get dressed.

"I knew I'd find yo' ass in here tryna escape." Looking up I saw Keisha and her big belly waddling into the room. Yea, Brandon had knocked her up and he had put my girl out of commission. I laughed lightly, knowing I had been caught.

"You got me. Who sent you up here anyway?" I asked, still preparing to get dressed.

"Nobody actually, I just came up here to visit and here it is you on your way out. Here, let me help you." She put her purse on the chair and helped me slip on an outfit Shawn had brought up for me last night.

"Thank you boo. I gotta get up outta this hospital. I've been in here one day too long. I need to see about TT asap." My face turned up just thinking about how I'd let that bitch get one up on me.

"I know yo' daddy gon' get in my ass behind me helping you leave here without him knowing. And Brandon, oh god he's gonna act like I went and gave birth on my own; extra as fuck." I laughed as she griped, but never stopped helping. When we were done I was fully dressed in a short set with the PLT logo on it. After checking myself out, I had Keisha drop me off to TT's apartment on Prospect Ave. in the Bronx. She tried to talk me out of coming until I was one hundred percent; this couldn't wait though. I went to step out of the car when she pulled me back. "Wait, wait, ain't that Emery with the black hoodie on coming out of the building?"

Quickly looking in that direction, I recognized my daughter who was speed walking to a Toyota Camry that she didn't own. Before I could get out and say anything the car sped off. I looked at Keisha with a face that showed utter confusion. What was she doing coming out of TT's building? Not waiting for an answer, I proceeded to get out the car, this time Keisha followed. Here I was tryna be sneaky and my own child had one up on me. I was able to get TT's house address from one of the girls who didn't like her on the block. She just happened to be visiting the hospital during my stay and expressed how fucked up it was what she did to me.

Taking the elevator up to the second floor, me and a really pregnant Keisha moved about the hallway looking for the apartment. Finding it, my intuition told me that the door would be unlocked, I was right. I didn't have my gun, but I didn't come empty-handed either. Grabbing my knife from my pocket I flicked it open. Initially I thought no one was home since it was so quiet, but I moved about the apartment deadly and quick.

"Oh shit," I heard Keisha whisper loudly toward the front of the apartment. Heading that way to see what was going on, I met her in the kitchen along with TT's body. She had been shot twice, once in the hand and once in the chest.

"Emery?" I said in more of a question than an answer.

Emery

Seeing my mom hit the ground I swear my life flashed before my eyes. My eyes grew wide as saucers and it seemed like I could see the fire leaving the gun. Running over to her, I hit the ground and kept reminding her to stay with me and expressed how much I needed her. Waiting for the ambulance to come seemed like forever. I didn't even see the lady who shot her being dragged away. We made it to the hospital and the doctors began to work on her immediately.

When she awoke I knew it was for a reason. My mother had endured backstabbing, jail and more than one attempt on her life. She wasn't lucky, she was blessed. I decided at that moment there was no way that I'd let anyone hurt her again. The day she sent us home I made a plan that I was gonna take care of TT myself.

"Pop, I need a gun," I said to my grandfather who I had been staying with at his request while my mom was in the hospital.

"A gun?"

"Yes, you know, for protection. With Mom recently being shot I wanna make sure I'm protected at all times."

"Is that right?" I knew he was trying to pull the real reason out of me, but there was no way I was telling him. I kept a straight face and so did he. "Okay, I'm gonna give you a gun. You're of age now and I've taught you how to protect yourself. Just know that with guns come responsibility. Are you ready to take that on?"

"Yes." I walked out of the house with a Glock 43 and headed to Porscha's house.

"Are you sure about this Emi?" Porscha asked with her voice filled with concern. We were in her room and I was telling her my plan to kill TT. Porscha was my best friend and we had secrets we'd take to the grave, and this one would be added to the list.

"I'm positive P. I almost lost my mom last week and that is a pain that I'm not ready to experience. I need your help friend." I hated to put her in this position, but I knew I couldn't pull this off on my own.

"I got you, what you need?" I broke the plan to her in detail, not missing anything. I was able to get info on TT with no problem. It's crazy what you can find online by just paying for a simple background check on someone. She nodded her head in understanding and we got ready to head out. It was still light outside which I was okay with. I figured TT would be more lax during the day with her guard down.

We rode in silence, Porscha in the driver's seat. Many thoughts went through my mind during the drive. The one that stuck out the most was what my mom would think if she knew about what I had set out to do. I hoped she never found out. When we arrived I told Porscha to park across from the building and a couple cars down. I set my timer on my Apple watch to fifteen minutes once I got out the car. Making sure my hoody was secure over my head, I opted out of taking the elevator and jogged up the two flights of steps to her apartment. Knocking on the door I kept my head down.

"Who is it?" TT barked. Stuck, I didn't know what to say so I said nothing in hopes that she'd open the door. Fuck, I hadn't planned as well as I thought. It must've been my lucky day though because as soon as I went to say fuck it, I heard locks being popped. I waited until the door was open enough for me to get in before I pushed her making her fall to the ground. "What the fuck!" she yelled, popping back up just as I closed the door. I followed as she walked backwards into a kitchen.

Seeing her reach for something on the counter, no words were spoken as I shot her in her hand. I made sure to grab a silencer when I selected the gun from my pop. She let out a muffled scream and I removed my hoody. Her eyes said she recognized me and that's what I wanted; this shit was personal. Aiming like my pop had taught me, I aimed and the bullet made contact with her chest. Once she fell I booked it out of the apartment, making sure to close the door using my hoody.

Reaching the last step I kept a steady pace until I made it to Porscha's Toyota Camry. Only then did I let out the breath I'd been holding. Porscha didn't even look at me, she just drove and didn't stop until we made it to my house. Running inside, I went straight to the bathroom and threw up. That air of confidence I once possessed went out the window once the deed was done.

"So how you feeling?" I heard my mom's voice and didn't even bother looking at her, she knew. I shrugged my shoulders instead. "Put words to that Emi Ice."

"I feel like I can guarantee that no one will hurt you again." Leaning down next to me my mom wiped my mouth and helped me up. "Where's Porscha?"

"I sent her home. Listen, I don't ever want you to think you have to protect me. It's my job to protect you Emery. Some things you just can't take back and you have to understand that killing someone is not easy. It may feel that way for the moment, but you relive that for the rest of your life."

"I understand Ma." She helped me into the shower, placing my clothes in a plastic bag and taking the gun from me. I made sure to wash three times and stepped out feeling a little better. Before I could get comfortable in bed my mom knocked and opened the door.

"Babygirl, the next time you wanna kill someone make sure to get a number for a clean-up crew. Don't worry, Mama took care of that," she said with a wink and closed the door behind her.

Epilogue

My daughter had caught her first and last body at seventeen years old. It's crazy how your life can get turned upside down unexpectedly. After that day, Emi and I never discussed what happened at TT's house, and we never would. Shawn questioned if I had anything to do with the murder and I was honest when I told him no. For the first time since being released I felt free. Free from attempts on my life and free to live it to the fullest.

Elijah had done a complete one eighty with me, and Emi was very instrumental in that. His outward disdain for me had subsided to the point where we could be in the same room with each other for more than a few minutes. I was happy about it because I had grown to love him like a son. Speaking of son, Shawn had kept his word and knocked me up; it was a good night. I often reflect to that day when I was shot and I had a moment in my mind with Eli Sr. It was needed and in a weird way I felt like he set me free that day.

"Babe, come on, everybody outside waiting on us," Shawn called out to me while entering our bedroom. Today was my baby shower. Our circle had gathered in my back yard to celebrate with us.

"Okay, here I come baby." He looked so handsome in his Burberry button-down and matching shorts. "You look so good."

"And you look edible. Come on, let me show you something real quick." He motioned towards the bathroom and I giggled.

"Oh no, no sir, everybody waiting on us, remember?" Wrapping my arms around his neck, I placed a simple kiss on his lips. "This is life."

The End

Note from Author: I really hope you all enjoyed the finale as much as I enjoyed writing it. I promise for the fifty times I got stuck (lol) I thought of your words of encouragement and pushed to get this book done in a timely manner. Thank you, thank you from the bottom of my heart. Until the next read. Xoxo, Nai

NOTE FROM AUTHOR

I really hope you all enjoyed the finale as much as I enjoyed writing it. I promise for the fifty times I got stuck (lol) I thought of your words of encouragement and push to get this book done in a timely manner. Thank you, thank you from the bottom of my heart. Until the next read. Xoxo, Nai

ABOUT THE AUTHOR

Nai McCrae is a Harlem, NY-bred woman with a pen that speaks with her NY flare. An author that will have you tickled with her quit wit and slick tongue, writing has always been her passion. A mother of three rambunctious children, her stories take her to another place. Intrigued by the beauty, emotion, and drama that comes with relationships, Nai has a keen ability to make her characters come alive right before your eyes. Blending real life and the fantasies that allow her to escape the day-to-day, Nai meshes the ordinary with the extraordinary, creating the perfect formula for the urban romance she's quickly becoming known for.

Royalty Publishing House is now accepting manuscripts from aspiring or experienced urban romance authors!

WHAT MAY PLACE YOU ABOVE THE REST:

Heroes who are the ultimate book bae: strong-willed, maybe a little rough around the edges but willing to risk it all for the woman he loves.

Heroines who are the ultimate match: the girl next door type, not perfect - has her faults but is still a decent person. One who is willing to risk it all for the man she loves.

The rest is up to you! Just be creative, think out of the box, keep it sexy and intriguing!

If you'd like to join the Royal family, send us the first 15K words (60 pages) of your completed manuscript to submissions@royaltypublishinghouse.com

LIKE OUR PAGE!

Be sure to LIKE our Royalty Publishing House page on Facebook!

CPSIA information can be obtained
at www.ICGtesting.com
Printed in the USA
LVHW041659220719
624869LV00006B/1070

9 781076 753946